The Cream of Devon

of Devon

An Anthology of Short Stories
From the County that Rhymes With Heaven

Copyright © Blue Poppy Publishing 2022

The copyrights to individual stories in this book remain with the respective authors as listed in the contents section. Blue Poppy Publishing has exclusive worldwide distribution rights under agreements with each author. All rights reserved. No part of this publication may be reproduced, distributed, or transmitted in any form or by any means, including photocopying, recording, or other electronic or mechanical methods, without the prior written permission of the author or the publisher, except in the case of brief quotations embodied in critical reviews, and certain other non-commercial uses where permitted by local legislation.

This is a work of fiction. All characters, places, and events related herein are fictional or are used in a fictional setting.

Edited by Sarah Dawes
Layout and Design by Oliver Tooley
Printed by Severn Print, Gloucester
Body font – Garamond 12pt
Title font –Brioso Pro – Baskerviille Old Face
Published by Blue Poppy Publishing, Devon
ISBN: 978-1-83778-000-6

Preface

The contents of this book come largely from entries to a short story competition run by Blue Poppy Publishing in 2022. I had several aims in this competition. Publicity was certainly one of them. The first prize was £250 (a fairly substantial sum for contests of this sort) and there was a further £250 in runner-up prizes up for grabs.

However, another reason for the competition was to discover (and nurture) some new writing talent in Devon. I believe we did so, with writers like Alex Morrison and Jade Ruby coming, seemingly, from nowhere and taking runner-up prizes.

The third reason was to provide material for Blue Poppy Publishing to move towards a more traditional publishing role, paying the writer for their work and covering the cost of publication, thereby also taking on the financial risk or reward as a legitimate business.

Following the competition, with almost – but not quite – enough excellent stories to fill a book, I opened submissions for other Devon-based writers to send their short stories to be included in an anthology. In addition, I have added one short story of my own, which I wrote as an experiment to see if I could write a short story within the rules of my own competition. It turns out I could not, as my story ran on to 6,000 words. I must respect the discipline of the writers who did keep under the 2,500-word limit.

At the end of the book you will find a brief biography and bibliography of the contributing writers. If you like their stories, you may want to check out their other books.

This book represents a considerable gamble for me personally. I hope, admittedly with considerable confidence, that you enjoy it and tell others about it as well.

Oliver (Olli) Tooley

Competition Winners

The judges awarded first place to Stand and Deliver, by Colin Smith. There were then five more stories which were too close to separate and so the remaining prize pot was divided equally between them. They were: Scone With the Wind and Pickled Cockles by Jade Ruby, Under the Spreading Oak by Jane Bheemah, Stand To by Alex Morrison, and Miss Emily Eden by Lalla Merlin. Congratulations to each of them and to everyone whose story made it into this book.

Preface	iii
Stand and Deliver – Colin Smith	1
The Cross – Oliver J Tooley	10
Stand-To – Alex Morrison	29
A Load of Rubbish – Katie Mallett	37
Raparee Beach – Caroline Berry	43
The Final Battle – Val Allsup	48
Scone With the Wind – Jade Ruby	52
Home Is Where the Heart Is – Maria Kinnersley	60
Dolores Goes Camping – Jade Ruby	66
The Bright Orange Swimming Hat – Irene Sugden	74
Soy Un Perdedor – Nathalie Denzey	81
Not a Royal Day Out – Ralph Bell-Ley	87
The Phoenix – Darren Colwill	94
A Roman in Devon – Darren Colwill	101
Under the Spreading Oak – Jane Bheemah	108
A Serene Affair – Ella-Jane Hobson	116
Partings – Pamela Vass	125
The Split: Before and After – Damien Mansfield	129
The Kelpie – Lalla Merlin	138
Miss Emily Eden – Lalla Merlin	142
Pickled Cockles – Jade Ruby	150
Author Biographies	158

Stand and Deliver
Colin Smith

"All they wealth!" Tom says. "I'll be rich in this cent'ry o' your'n, bey."

He's staring at a young woman: short, blonde, and with a riot of piercings in ears, nose and chin. I'd estimate the lot to come to, oh, a fiver? Claire's finest, if not Poundland's. Hardly Cartier. More horse and cartier, really.

Speaking of horse, Tom kicks into Winnie's flanks and starts heading towards the young woman. "Oh, no, no, no!" I shout, grabbing at his leg to stop him. "Don't you know who that is?"

It's a stupid thing to say, as I don't know who she is myself. But I have to make something up quick, or the populace of Barnstaple might hear some very loud screaming shortly, quite likely followed by sirens.

He stares at my hand, then into my face. I let go, post-haste. The phrase 'if looks could kill' might well have been invented for him. And even if looks can't, his twin flintlock pistols, which I've insisted he hides under his cloak (as if that doesn't make him stand out enough in a crowd), undoubtedly can.

"No, bey, I've no idea who she be."

Fortunately, I've had a second or two to indulge in some wild improvisation. "Oh. Well … Have you not heard of the Thieftaker of Barnstaple?"

He raises an eyebrow. "The Thieftaker o' Barnstaple?"

"Oh, yes. The Thieftaker. Notorious throughout the whole of North Devon nowadays, the Thieftaker is. Never been known to miss an arrest. And anyone touches his daughter, well …"

The other eyebrow joins the first by his hairline. "This maid, then, she be 'is daughter?"

"Oh, absolutely she be – er … is," I say, wondering where exactly I'm going with this, and wishing it was anywhere but here. "Eldest of two – er … seven. The other six, brothers. All giants, all following their father's profession. Not ones to mess around with, the Thieftaker and his family. Believe me."

I hold my breath, hoping he will believe me.

If he had a third eyebrow, I'm sure it would be joining the other two, such is the look of scepticism he's aiming at me. (Unless it's wind. But that smell's more likely to be the horse, thinking about it.)

"And this Thieftaker's name be what, bey? So's I might know if I come across 'im?"

"His name?"

Oh, heck. Come on, quick, a name – think of a name … Thank the stars (the Hollywood ones in particular), inspiration strikes. "His name is Johnny – I mean, Jonathan – Depp. The Pirate of the Caribbean, they call him. When they're not calling him the Thieftaker of Barnstaple, of course," I end rather lamely, wondering if I've gone a little too far.

To my great relief, it seems to satisfy him. He loses interest in the girl, and studies the Sticklepath roundabout again. He's very attracted by the stones. They remind him of his true love's teeth, apparently.

I haven't a clue who decided to send Tom Faggus, Devon's most famous highwayman, nearly 400 years forward into the twenty-first century. Some malevolent sorcerer or something – has to have been. First I knew about it was when I received a text from my Uncle Alex a few hours ago: 'I've got a weirdo on the bus'.

Alex owns and operates his own coach service, going up and down the country between here and wherever. I've never known exactly, and I'm not sure he knows, quite where he is half the time. It's a sort of National Express for the desperate, implicit in his advertising slogan: 'I take you where you want to go, or more likely somewhere else, but at least you'll be able to get to where you want to go from there with only a small amount of trouble – and anyway, I'm cheaper than the train.'

I texted back: 'Isn't that what buses are for, attracting weirdos?'

His reply was on my screen almost before I'd hit send. Uncle Alex knows he shouldn't use the phone when driving, but he never has been one for sticking to the rules. Or the speed limit, when he can get away with it. You know that thing on Star Wars about the Kessel Run? Alex once hit three times light-speed between Bradford and Luton. The passengers got home two hours before they left. Han Solo would've been wetting himself.

'This weirdo's different', the reply said. 'He's brought a horse on with him'.

Ah. Now that was too good to miss.

I don't have much work on at the minute, so I got to Tiverton to meet them with no problem. I knew Uncle Alex's coach was on its way minutes before it arrived. That much screaming tends to carry.

He didn't so much draw up at the stop as allow nature – and the kerb – to take its course. The doors opened and disgorged a crowd of white-faced, crying, shaking entities that might have once been human beings. "He's back there," Alex gestured towards the rear.

I looked. And then looked again. "You said he'd brought his horse with him," I said. "Not that he was actually riding it."

"Been like that since I picked him up at six this morning. Apparently, some prat laughed at his get-up and started calling him Dick Turpin. When he found out who that was – and after the prat had been carted off to hospital – he decided he wanted to better that 200-mile-ride Turpin's supposed to have made. I happened to be waiting here, so he stuck a pistol in my face and demanded I take him to York. I told him it was Plymouth or nothing, so he bought a day return and he's been sitting back there ever since. I told him that even if he does the 200 miles, it doesn't count if the horse's legs aren't moving, but he was too busy robbing everybody of their loose change to take any notice. Bet that was going to be my whip-round, as well. See what you can do with him."

The horse came clip-clopping along the aisle, then manoeuvred itself down the steps onto ground level. He (the rider, not the horse – that turned out to be female, so will hereafter be referred to as she/her) stared down at me. "Who be you, bey?"

I held out my hand. "Garry Marsh. I've been sent to meet you, Mr ... er ... ?"

He looked at my hand as if wondering whether to shake it or bite it off, so I put it away to use again later on. He stared around at the scenery, if that's the right word for a bus station by a Marks and Spencer's, and said, "Strange place ye have 'ere, Garry

Marsh. I be Thomas Faggus. Tom to me friends – but ye can call I Mr Faggus."

So I did. And, thanks to Alex, who skedaddled for a Costa as soon as my back was turned, I've been lumbered with him the rest of the day.

I brought him back to Barnstaple as soon as I could, though he insisted I wait till he finished robbing the contingent waiting for the 155. He was impressed with the carrier bag of ready meals he pinched off one of them; the Chinese Foo Yung Noodles he declared to be, "Best worms I ever tasted."

He did complain about the lack of opportunity to perform any hold-ups on his travels with Alex. "Can't do 'im with they glass winder-things there, bey. Them can't hear me cries of 'Stand and Deliver!' I does a good 'Stand and Deliver', I does. Ye should see the maids' bosoms heave when they 'ear it."

He stared across at a couple of long-haired lads lounging around by the back of Argos: leftovers from the 1970s, by the look of them. "Don't maids be 'avin' bosoms these days?"

He insisted we travel properly, rather than, "inside one of they 'orseless things," he said. "Winnie kept wantin' to sit on some bey's lap and look out the winder. That be not natural."

So it was that I found myself mounted on his horse's rear, clinging tight to his waist, and trying not to think of the effect the journey was having on my piles. As we galloped up the A361, I had to persuade him not to brandish his pistols at every passing Ford Fiesta. Not that he would have had much luck in the stand and deliver department with them, I don't suppose; if Ford drivers had any wealth at all, they'd probably be Volkswagen drivers.

"What be all these gestures with the two fingers they keep givin' us?" he asked at one point.

I thought quickly again, not wanting the pistols to reappear. "I think they're saying it's two miles to the next waypoint. We use them for parking so the kids can get out for a wee."

"Be that so? We just do that while we be ridin'. Saves time."

I sat as far behind him as I could without sliding off after that.

Once in Barnstaple, I conducted him on the grand tour. He was impressed with the town centre, but I had to move him on quickly after he tried to hold up a pensioner on a mobility scooter. We took in Bear Street (he confessed himself disappointed by the lack of bears), then he shot a couple of seagulls from the new bridge and stowed them away, 'for dinner, which I'll be 'avin' dreckly', and finally we ended up here, at Sticklepath roundabout. He was instantly taken by the stones, as I say. And the traffic lights. "You say they'm stop all they carriages wi' no messin' about chasin' they?"

"That's right," I confirmed after I'd finished processing all they – I mean, those – 'theys'. "But only when the red light's showing. That doesn't mean, though, that when the green one's on you're allowed to gallop alongside people yelling, 'Your money or your life.' Especially the carriages with the blue flashing lights and sirens. We're lucky he was in a hurry."

"What about that big one over there, though, bey? Why was him tellin' me it were another two miles to somewhere?"

The big one he's talking about has stopped on the triangular island the other side of the roundabout, and is disgorging brown gunk onto the ground from its tipped-up rear end. Tom watches this in fascination.

"Come on," I say. "I want to show you the museum before it shuts. They might have something about you in there."

He waves an impatient hand. "No, bey. I wanna watch the thing wi' they little black bags again."

"Sorry?" Then I realise what he's talking about. "No," I explain, "that was a man picking up after his dog. This is an aggregate lorry unloading soil. Two different things."

"Oh." He shrugs. "Pity. I were lookin' forward to seeing 'ow many bags it be takin'."

He urges Winnie forwards, towards the lorry. Startled, I hesitate, then follow, wondering why he might be heading in that direction and fearing a lot of immediate trouble because of it – trouble for me, that is.

Once there, the reason becomes apparent. I cover my face with my hands, and hope to God the lorry driver hasn't noticed.

My prayer isn't answered. "Oi. What the bloody hell're you doing?"

I really don't know where the horse is getting it all from. I mean, we left any number of steaming deposits behind us during the journey from Tiverton, and at various points round the town centre, and now she's standing and delivering again – big-time.

"You talkin' to I, bey?"

The driver climbs down from his cab and clumps towards us, rolling up his shirtsleeves. He has very impressive biceps, I notice.

"Yes, I'm talking to you! And I want to know what the *bleep* you think you're letting your *bleep* horse do all over my *bleep* load!'

I have to explain at this juncture that I've censored his speech somewhat. Delicate eyes might be reading.

"Just addin' to it," Tom says, as if it's the most commonplace thing in the world; which it probably is in his world, come to think of it. "If you'm not be goin' to pick 'im up in they little bags, Winnie may as well make use of 'im."

I decide to interpose. It's either that, or leg it like fun in the other direction and leave the police to clean up the aftermath.

"Just a misunderstanding," I tell the driver. "My friend's from Ilfracombe. I'm sure that explains things."

"Nevertheless," the driver says, "they need that soil for a new road surface."

"Oh," I say. "I thought a new surface had only just been put down?"

"It has. But this dirt's for a surface to replace the one my lorry's just torn up delivering this dirt. We do that every few weeks. It's a self-perpetuating thing. Keeps us in jobs."

"I see," I say. Up close, those biceps really are impressive, and the old phrase 'discretion is the better part of valour' springs to mind. "Come on, Mr Faggus. Probably time to go."

He waves me away. "No, bey. I wanna know what this gurt noodle be goin' to do now he'm started."

Ah. For 'discretion', read 'stupidity'. I cover my eyes again. "I really think it's time to go," I venture.

"Oh, no," the driver says. "I want to know what laddo here's going to do with his cap guns."

Cap … Oh!

I uncover my eyes. Tom has, indeed, whipped out his flintlocks and is brandishing them at the driver. Things have now, I feel, gone some way beyond passing off as 'just a misunderstanding'.

The driver is laughing his head off – and I wish that was literally true, because 'has had his head shot off' (as is likely to happen any minute) sounds rather more gruesome.

"I warn ye, bey," Tom is saying.

"Ha ha," the driver replies.

Oh, hell, I think.

There's a click. Two clicks. We all three stare down at Tom's pistols.

"Blast!" Tom says. "Them always does that when I don't want 'em to. They powder must be damp."

"Why don't you just *bleep* off?" the driver snarls. To my immense relief, he turns away and stomps back to his cab rather than laying about Tom's body – or, more importantly, mine.

The soil having long finished spilling out of the lorry (and Winnie's backside, for that matter), he rights his dumper and drives away, waving a final 'two miles' at us as he leaves.

Tom's still staring despondently at his pistols. "I'm be 'avin' to clean they damn things out now," he mutters.

I take a chance and clap him on the shoulder. "Never mind," I say. "I'm sure no good would have come of it anyway."

"Look, Mr Faggus," I add, trying to cheer him up, "the Thieftaker's daughter's still over there. I think her dad's on holiday at the moment, and those brothers I spoke about aren't really that big …"

The Cross
Oliver J Tooley

The warm, flickering, amber glow of a real log fire dominated the ambience in the Plough this evening, as it had done on countless evenings since the place had first been built over 300 years ago. The scent of waxed cotton jackets mingled with the woodsmoke and flowing Exmoor Gold, while the ebb and flow of conversation and laughter filled the ears. Bill, Harry, and John sat around the dark, circular wooden table, with its heavy cast iron base. Their ruddy beer glasses glinted and pulsed in the firelight as if they were imbued with magical properties. In a way it was magic, just sitting there, first pint already downed, letting the muscles relax after a hard day spreading slurry. In some ways little had changed in all those centuries. True, they now had a John Deere the size of a small cottage with the power of a couple of hundred shire horses, and even Harry, the eldest of the three, had a slim, shiny, black smartphone in his pocket, even if he did only use it to let the wife know he was on his way home for tea.

The door opened, letting a cold draught whip around the bar until it shut again with a clatter and the wind, losing momentum, settled down to sleep somewhere in the middle of the floor. The newcomers were youngsters, three of them, late teens or early twenties, woolly hats and fleece jackets, wearing trainers, not wellies. They were chatting animatedly on arrival, continuing a conversation that had started outside.

"I dunno, Lunnen, or Brizzle, I guess. Nothin' ever 'appens here, thass for sure!"

"You wouldn't last five minutes in London, Dave, they'd eat you for breakfast."

There was laughter as the lads got to the bar and ordered. The lass serving them, Sal by name, smiled warmly at Dave, who failed to notice. They sat at an empty table near the fire and acknowledged the three older men.

"Alright Dad?" Dave said to Bill.

"Alright son? You'm still on about movin' then?"

"Well …" he hesitated.

"You thought about work? Not much call for a farm hand wi' a BTEC in animal care round Chelsea way, so I 'ear."

There was a ripple of laughter among the older group.

"Dave's right though," said one of the youngsters, coming to his friend's defence, "Nothing ever happens round 'ere."

"Oh, I dunno, bey," piped up John, "I 'eared tell of a ewe 'az juss give birth to a two-'eaded lamb."

"Get on! Wherezat to, then?" Harry asked.

"High Tree Farm, so uz tole."

"Never!"

"Tiz true!"

"So what're we doin' sittin' roun' suppin' ale. Drink up; lez get o'er there an' zee un."

Dave remained unconvinced and unimpressed. "There ain't no way no two-'eaded lamb's been born roun' yere. T'would've bin all over the internet by now."

"More's the point," cut in another of the youths, "Oi juss bin up at High Tree earlier an' nobody said a word."

"They'z keepin' it under they hats, innum," said John, tapping his rosy nose, a cheeky twinkle playing around his grey eyes.

"Garn, geddaway! You'm pulling uz plonkers, y'old devil!"

There were laughs all around as it became clear that John had indeed been pulling everyone's plonkers, but it gave them all an excuse to sup some more Exmoor or Carling as their tastes dictated.

The door opened again. The sleeping breeze awoke and went for a mad race around the pub while it had the chance. The newcomer was alone and the whole pub went quiet as they entered. It wasn't the fact that they were black that was remarkable. True, most folk round these parts were white, or at least rubicund, but there were other ethnicities represented in the village. There was a black graphic designer and his family, who had bought the old post office building, an Indian doctor who worked at North Devon District Hospital. Heck, even Sal behind the bar was of mixed heritage. No, what made this person look unusual was that they wore a floor-length black leather cloak topped off with a tricorn hat sporting a jaunty blue feather.

Undaunted by the obvious chill in the atmosphere, they walked to the bar, each step accompanied by a clink-clink sound that was uncomfortably loud in the unnatural silence. They ordered a Bloody Mary in a velvet voice that could have been a high tenor or a deep contralto. Sal told the stranger how much it was, and they drew back the cloak to reveal a powder-blue leather coin pouch tied to a gold waistband. From this, deft fingers in cream-gloved hands withdrew a coin.

Over by the fireplace, Harry muttered to the younger lads, "Nothin' ever 'appens 'ere, beys."

Sal looked at the glint of gold with a suspicious eye. She turned to call Tom, the landlord, but he was already on her shoulder. By no means an expert numismatist, Tom looked at the coin held in Sal's hand. It glinted gold but that didn't mean squat these days. A Quality Street toffee penny was shinier, and he had half a tin of them left over from Christmas. He picked it up and bit it. The stranger looked at him as though he were a complete idiot. Tom eyed the stranger and there followed an internal 'full and frank' discussion between the Tom who wanted to throw the stranger out immediately, and the Tom who often bought a scratch-card with his change, on the off-chance that this could be the big one.

The latter Tom won.

"I can't change this," he said.

"Keep it," the stranger replied, adding, "I need rooms in this town. Is this an inn or just a tavern?"

Tom's mind tried to fit the village of Shepherdfordsworth, (pronounced Sheppeth) inside the word 'town' and found, despite its lengthy name, that it rattled around too much. As to the question of his pub's status, he did a passable impression of a drowning fish as he tried to work out the correct answer.

"You'd be payin' wi' them little coins there, would 'ee?"

"That's the plan."

"Gimme five minutes."

Tom went back into the private area and picked up the telephone.

"Hello? ... Nicki, do you still collect coins an' that? ... That's more or less what I mean, yeah ... Yeah? Proper job! I don't s'pose you're about and can get over to the Plough roight now can 'ee? ... Yeah roight now, quick as possible ... Oi got summat I want you to 'ave a look at, see?"

He replaced the receiver. Nicki was a bit of an amateur archaeologist who had been a full-time librarian, now retired. Since she could walk to the pub in five minutes but would more likely cycle, Tom waited by the side door to keep an eye out for her. Once inside with decent light she examined the coin briefly.

"Did you bite this?"

"Well, thass how you test if 'eez gold, innum?"

"Pillock! There's tooth marks on it now. Still worth a bloody fortune. Where d'you find it?"

"I nev …" he stopped as he thought about the ma …. the wo … the person in the leather cloak with a whole bag of coins, each potentially worth a fortune, that they were planning on spending on a room, and perhaps more drinks. The thought took a split second. He continued, " … ver did go through them old boxes in the back cellar, 'till today, and that coin wuz in one of 'em. Thanks Nicki, you've been a tremendous help."

"Dunno what were so urgent you had to drag me over here at a moment's notice, though," she huffed, as she remounted her bike and cycled the couple of minutes back home.

Back in the bar, Tom did his best hotelier routine. "Would sir be after the deluxe suite or an economy room?"

Sal mouthed, "What deluxe suite?" at him from a position out of the stranger's line of sight. Then she had a further thought: what bloody economy room?

He waved her away.

"I'll take the deluxe – and it's madam if you don't mind! Aspen Delcroix." She proffered a hand.

"Ideal!" said Tom, reaching out to shake it. Then, thinking perhaps he ought to be more … gentlemanly, he added, "Charmed, Oi'm sure." He tentatively squeezed a couple of fingers. He wasn't sure if he was supposed to kiss the hand, but thankfully Ms Delcroix withdrew it before he came to any conclusions.

There were three bedrooms in the Plough: his own ensuite, which he had rashly offered as the 'deluxe', Sal's room, because the job had to be live-in when you didn't finish kicking folks out until long gone three in the morning some nights, and a spare room, which contained a lot of boxes and junk.

After a rapid sotto voce argument with Sal, it was agreed that he, Tom, would have to sleep in the junk room, although she agreed to help clear the boxes out of the way. Between frantic removals backstage and serving in the bar, the pair managed to arrange things so that Ms Delcroix could be made comfortable in Tom's room.

In the warm amber glow of the bar, Aspen Delcroix assessed the locals. Some still eyed her suspiciously, others had returned attention to their own conversations and drinks. Her eyes lighted on Dave and his friends. She walked over to their table.

"I'm looking for a man."

Dave managed not to spit out his drink.

There was a raucous shout from Harry at the next table, "Best come over 'ere maid; them's nobbut beys."

She glanced at the older group. "I need one who doesn't creak when he stands up."

The younger group all reacted with comments like "Shade!" "Ooh!" and "Burn!"

The lads took an immediate liking to the woman, which was not dulled by her striking, if rather masculine, looks.

"I might be available for some manly duties," Dave admitted, attempting nonchalance.

"Yes, you'll do. Come with me." Ms Delcroix strode from the pub.

Dave, hesitating at first, quickly decided he had better catch up or lose his job, whatever it was. Outside, he saw Ms Delcroix standing beside an oversized wooden trunk and a heavy leather travelling bag. There was no sign of a cab or other vehicle, but Dave assumed it had just left.

"You take the trunk upstairs to my room; I can manage the bag."

She picked up the bag and headed inside. Dave attempted to lift the trunk and collapsed on top of it. He steeled himself for another attempt and, forewarned, lifted it with some difficulty and followed his employer. He hadn't even asked if he was getting paid. There were ironic cheers for Dave's manful efforts as he lumbered the chest awkwardly past the bar and into the back area of the pub. He didn't dare rest it or let on how much he was struggling while his mates, and his dad's mates, could see, but once out of sight he stopped for a breather at the foot of the stairs. After lugging the trunk into the room and dumping it at the foot of the bed, he did his best to get his breath back without looking like the effort had almost killed him.

"You're strong; I like that. I may need you again for something rather more challenging." Ms Delcroix handed him a copper coin. Dave didn't look at it.

"More challenging like a bigger case? Or more challenging like …" Dave didn't have any ideas that he thought would be appropriate.

Aspen Delcroix looked at Dave and seemed to make a quick character judgement. She stepped past him, a waft of orange blossom enveloping him briefly. She glanced outside and then closed the door. Dave swallowed hard and tried to suppress his most optimistic thoughts.

"What do you know about demons?"

Dave's face experimented with a number of expressions; it tried surprised, quizzical, confused, contemplative, and calculating in quick succession. After a pause he said, "Kinda fiery things that live in hell?"

"Not always fiery. You could call it hell if you want. It's a bit more complex than that, but sure, yes, demons. What do you know about them?"

Dave began, "That they don't …" and then his brain caught up with his mouth and asked for a brief discussion in private.

It said, "If you're about to say they don't exist, could we consider the possibility that this … let's call her handsome … woman, who smells nice, and who is alone with you in her bedroom, might think they do, and the possibility exists that if you say the wrong thing, she might ask you to leave? And, by the way, I am not the only one here who is thinking along these lines."

Dave adjusted his thoughts and started again. "Well, demons are … evil, and very, very … bad."

As speeches go, Dave realised he was not up there with Martin Luther King, or Churchill. He decided to shut up until he had something intelligent to say.

Aspen Delcroix began to explain. "Demons are evil entities that exist for no discernible purpose. They are manifestations of utter chaos and evil. They destroy life and order wherever they find it. For the most part, they are kept in a plane of existence called the Abyss, but sometimes the boundaries between the material world and the Abyss become thin and there is a rift between worlds. My job is to travel to the place and time of the rift, destroy any demons that pass through, and to close the rift afterwards."

Dave stuck with his decision to keep quiet unless he had something sensible to say. His silence was rewarded with more information.

"I need someone from the local time and region to help me. You know the area, I know demons. Got it?"

"Got it, yeah. So these demons …?"

"I think you only have a small incursion here. Nothing worse than Vzzghrt." It sounded like she was choking.

"Do you want a glass of water?"

Ms Delcroix impatiently waved the suggestion aside.

"What …? No, thank you, I'm fine. Now, Vzzghrt. It's a small demon. It flies. Think of a big blowfly but with a sting."

"We've got a zapper at home; Mum uses it in the kitchen."

"No need. We've got what we need in here." She opened the trunk, revealing a variety of strange apparatus. The colours were a mixture of brass, silver, black, and glowing electric blue. "You have to keep this to yourself. The fewer locals that know, the better."

Dave nodded. No bugger would believe him anyway.

Aspen Delcroix glanced at a small device on her belt. It went *ping* rather in the manner of an old-fashioned striking clock announcing one o'clock. "Come on then." She lifted two larger devices from the trunk and handed one to Dave. It was some sort of handle, like a large sword hilt with no blade. It hummed gently in his hand.

"What, right now?" Dave asked.

"The rift is not far from here. The image I have is of an old-looking barn with a tiled roof. In front is a tall, straight tree with no branches, and a very small building, bright red, with lots of glass windows all round."

Dave tried to interpret the description. He couldn't think of any small red buildings.

"How small is this red building?"

Aspen Delcroix indicated a width by holding her hands about three feet apart, and jumped, pointing with her hand to indicate a height of about eight feet. "Actually a little taller than that, like the height of this ceiling."

Dave wracked his brains. He tried a different tack. "This tree – really straight, no branches?" He recalled there was an old pine growing out on the Barum road that had been trimmed over many years and was pretty straight.

"Yes, it is a strange tree. There are some small branches. They are a different colour from the trunk: black, and regular shaped. Evenly spaced on either side of the tree."

Dave slumped. This didn't sound like any tree he'd ever seen.

"You sure you're in the right place?"

"Certain. The red building, it has something inside it, you can see through the glass. A yellow box on one wall. Oh, and there's a word written on the side of the building, I don't know the word."

Light dawned for Dave.

"Defibrillator?"

"Yes!"

"Come on, I know where we're going." He headed for the door.

"Not that way!" Ms Delcroix headed for the window. She opened it, looked down, climbed out and dropped onto the ground fifteen feet below, landing like a wobbly gymnast.

Dave looked down without enthusiasm. But he didn't want to look weak. He climbed out and then, grabbing hold of the window frame, lowered himself until he was dangling from the ledge. It was still a fair drop, and he would scrape on the wall the whole way down. He prepared himself and pushed away from the wall a bit as he dropped. The barest hint of disdain crossed Aspen Delcroix's face as she helped him get up from the ground.

"Which way?"

Dave led off down a narrow lane lined with hedgerows. "It's not far. Less than a mile."

Bright headlights approached and the two moved out of the way, Aspen making sure the devices they were carrying were not visible to the driver as they passed.

They reached the old telephone box which, rather pointlessly considering its location, had now been fitted with a defibrillator. Next to it was a telegraph pole. Behind that was the old barn. The small device on Aspen Delcroix's belt was pinging now like a clock striking midnight. Dave could see that something was definitely not right. From the barn came a worrying crimson glow, the light spilling out through cracks in roof tiles and in the old cob walls. He could hear a fizzing, crackling sound and there was a burning metallic smell in the air, like the morning after fireworks night.

"Come on." Aspen moved towards the large double doors where spears of reddish light were stabbing through gaps in the frames. "Get behind me and take out any that get past." She hauled open the big door and swung the device at the first of the creatures that flew towards her.

When she had said 'like a big blowfly', Dave had not imagined this. It was larger than a tennis ball and resembled a glowing ember with wings and a vicious-looking barbed proboscis. He hesitated, transfixed. Aspen slashed left and right; whips of electric blue and white light emerged from the handle of the weapon, taking down several demons in a few swipes. When hit, the glowing, buzzing demons burst with radiant white light and vapourised. One got past Aspen and headed for Dave.

"Don't let it get away! And don't let it sting you either!" she yelled.

Animated by her shout, Dave launched his weapon at the creature. Nothing happened.

"Squeeze the handle as you swing!" Aspen added, flicking several more demons to oblivion. "There are too many of them! I'm going to close the doors until we can think of another plan."

Slashing all about her, she tried to get the door closed but in doing so let several more get past her. Dave wasn't going to screw this up again. He was not going to let a bunch of demons, with a name that sounded like a cat bringing up a furball, run amok in his village. Besides, Ms Delcroix smelled of orange blossom and she was the best-looking woman that Dave had ever noticed paying him any attention. He was not the most observant when it came to subtle social signals.

Gripping his unfamiliar weapon like his life depended on it, which it almost certainly did, he began to lay about him as he had seen his boss do. While Ms Delcroix forced the doors shut, Dave slashed and dashed, taking down half a dozen of these fiendish Vzzghrt things. Only one remained – the first escapee – and it danced tantalisingly out of his reach, zipping and buzzing this way and that, moving away from him over the hedgerow. He had to stop it. He leapt up the bank, encountering a mass of tangled brambles, and scrambled up onto the hedge of hazel and quickthorn. He tried to ignore the pain, focused on keeping this evil thing from reaching his friends and family. He managed to reach the top of the hedge, despite his hands bleeding and the rips in his jeans, and lashed at the buzzing ball of hatred taunting him. He missed and fell down along the hedge-top, the weapon flung from his grip. The Vzzghrt saw its chance and swooped down, buzzing with fiendish delight.

In his remaining seconds Dave found enough time to think, "Well that's the end of my demon-hunting career." The barbed proboscis grew rapidly larger as it bore down on him, the body behind it glowing evilly. Just as he steeled himself for the anticipated agonising pain there was a flash of blue light, and the demon was blasted away. He could smell a metallic tang, mingled with what he had to assume was the smell of his own eyebrows burning. He could live with that. He looked at Aspen Delcroix, who was far too far away to have used the same weapon he was wielding. Sure enough, there was something in her hand that was still sparking electric blue.

"Thanks," he said, unable to load the word with as much gratitude as he currently felt.

"No problem." She pulled a similar weapon from her belt and handed it to him. "Plane-shift blaster. Use sparingly; it doesn't hold much charge. Oh – and don't miss!"

"What does it do?"

"It sends anyone or anything you hit back to the Abyss."

"Anyone?"

"Anyone!"

Dave eyed the weapon with a deep, and fully justified, mistrust.

"Right, are you ready?" she said, looking at the broiling doors.

"Ready? I thought we were going to come up with another plan?"

"I just did. We're going in there and closing the doors. If we win, we walk out of there alive; if we lose …"

Dave looked aghast. "If we lose?"

"Oh, if we lose you won't be dead, you'll be one of them!" With a look of grim determination, she turned to open the doors.

"Wait! If we lose, we turn into demons?"

"A succinct summary. Yes."

She turned her attention to the door handle again and paused as Dave said, "So …"

"So we had better not lose, right?" She opened the door and stepped in, her electric-blue whip flashing about her, followed by Dave aping her movements. He closed the door behind him.

The full-beam headlights and unnecessary fog-lamps of a passing car swept across the phone box, the defibrillator glowing yellow in the beams. The driver did not notice the flashes of blue and red emanating from the derelict barn behind. After a matter of scarcely two minutes, which felt to the human occupants of the barn like hours, the doors burst open and Aspen Delcroix emerged on all fours, gasping for breath. She was followed by Dave, only slightly less traumatised by the experience.

As he got back his breath he muttered, "Proper job," then gave a brief snort of relieved laughter. "That was fun," he lied.

Aspen collapsed and rolled onto her back.

"Are you alright?" Dave began but knew before he had finished that she was not. There was an amoeboid patch of darkness spreading across the deep blue of her shirt.

"I've been hit. Listen, get back to the trunk. There's a brass cylinder about this long and this wide." She indicated the size with her hands. "Fetch it. I should have brought it with me. I'm such a fool!" She flinched with the pain.

"Shouldn't I call an ambulance?" Dave asked.

"What in all the hells would an ambulance do for a demon sting?" Aspen groaned, then, "Hurry!" she hissed through gritted teeth.

Dave stood up and ran along the lane back to the pub, his thoughts racing. It would take him maybe five or six minutes to run the mile back to the pub, and more like ten to make the return journey. He didn't know how long it would take to find and retrieve the cylinder, but Aspen would be writhing in agony for a quarter of an hour at best. As he approached the pub he began to think about how he would get in and out without raising suspicion. He looked at himself. He had looked worse, but only after a particularly bad day on one of the muckier jobs on the farm. And he was still carrying a brass and silver electric-blue whip and a plane-shift blaster.

He investigated the window where they had climbed out earlier. There was an enormous red Massey Fergusson parked right beneath it. Dave offered up a silent prayer of thanks to the owner for ignoring the request not to park there, as he clambered up the great beast and onto the roof, which brought him level with the window. Within a few moments he was climbing back down, leaping from the footplate and off down the lane again, the cylinder clutched tightly in his fist.

Breathless and nursing a painful stitch, he reached Aspen's side. She had managed to bandage the wound while he'd been gone. She had stopped the flow of blood but was still clinging to life by a thread. She held out her hand for the cylinder. Dave handed it to her and then took it back when he saw she was unable to unscrew the lid.

"Take out one of the rods," she grunted. "Careful – don't press the ends. It's a poison antidote."

Dave removed one of a number of thin golden rods from the cylinder and handed it to Aspen. She grasped it. With closed eyes, she felt along its length and then placed one end against the skin on her forearm pushing against the other end with her thumb. The rod shortened visibly, and a tiny pearl of blood appeared on her skin at the point of contact. She smiled and fell back with a satisfied sigh. Dave took off his jacket, rolled it up, and placed it under her head.

"Give me a minute, then can you help me get back to the inn?" she said.

Dave indicated that he would – once again, his words and gestures inadequate to convey how fervently he wanted to help.

It took half an hour to walk the mile back to the pub. As they approached, Dave hoped that the red Fergie was still there and, if it was, that Aspen would be strong enough to climb up it. It was there and Aspen drew on inner strength that Dave could only dream of to get back through the window. She threw off her leather cloak and collapsed on the bed, an exhausted, dishevelled wreck. Dave wasn't much better, but now he started to laugh uncontrollably, sinking down with his back to the wall. Despite the pain, this started Aspen laughing as well. They had been, figuratively although not literally, through hell and somehow you either had to laugh or cry, so they laughed until they cried.

There was a knock on the door followed by a concerned-looking Sal.

"Are you alright? You've been absolutely ages with that trunk," she was saying as she entered. Her eyes took in the partly undressed woman on the bed and Dave in an almost foetal position on the floor, both of them looking dishevelled in the extreme.

"What happened? Did the trunk fight back?" She looked now at the trunk, which Dave had left open. The strange tools and weapons glinted back at her.

"It's not what it looks like," Dave said. Internally, an incredulous voice said, "It's not what it looks like? What is this, some dreadful farce?" He went on, "I mean, there's nothing weird going on here ..." He looked around the room and tried to think of anything, anything at all, that could possibly be any more weird than this. Perhaps if they were dressed as clowns? Or if the trunk was filled with shark-infested custard?

Sal turned to leave. "I don't know what's going on and I don't think I want to know. What two consenting adults get up to in private is their own business." She looked pretty hurt though.

Aspen laughed loudly and said, "Wait, young lady. Whatever you think this is, it is definitely nothing between this young man and me."

Sal put her hands on her hips and stared at Aspen, her face radiating suspicion.

Aspen sat up, wincing as she did so. "This young man has been helping me to deal with an incursion of ... uninvited guests."

Sal's mistrustful expression remained unmoved.

"There's no romance whatsoever between us, I assure you."

Dave made an involuntary sound that betrayed a teeny bit of disappointment.

"Really, David?" Aspen laughed briefly. "I am well over 300 years old."

It was Sal's turn to snort derisively. "What's your secret, Oil of Olay?"

Dave, who had seen the Vzzghrt and wielded the weapons in the chest, was more open to new ideas, but even he baulked at this. "Three hundred? You don't look a day over thirty," he said, thinking she could easily be forty.

"Well, looks can be deceiving," Aspen said. "Look, the game is definitely up for me with Sal, here. She knows something's not right and if we don't tell her the truth then whatever we do tell her will be worse. Besides, if you're going to be my eyes and ears on the ground here to guard against future incursions then your girlfriend had better be clued into what's going on."

"Wait – she's not my girlfriend," Dave protested.

"She isn't? Well then all I can say is you're nowhere near as smart as I thought you were. She certainly has eyes for you!"

Sal wasn't sure whether to be annoyed or to laugh. Dave looked at her and she smiled back. It was painfully awkward but, at the same time, it was obvious that Aspen's instinct was spot on. It could wait, however.

Dave turned to Aspen, "What do you mean eyes and ears on the ground?"

"I can't stay here. The incursion has been sealed off, for now. But if the fabric between planes is thin then there will be more. I need you to keep an eye out. I said I wanted to keep this between as few people as possible, but two pairs of eyes and ears are better than one, and if you two are going to be an item there's no way you, David, can keep this secret from Sal. So, what do you say? Are you willing to help?"

Sal looked at Dave and indicated with a nod that she would go along with his decision. She hadn't seen what they might be up against, but it sounded like they would be on the right side.

"Well, yeah, I guess," Dave said. "Where are you going then?"

"I told you, I have to go all over the world and to all points in time to deal with incursions."

"What, like the whole world and all time? How do you cope?"

"Well, it's not just me; there's a whole team of us. And it's mostly only human history. If demons come through before that … well, I don't know. We don't go there. Too many variables."

"Do I get one of those plane-shift blasters?"

"No you do not, David! But you do get these."

"What are these, then?"

"This one is a demon detector." She handed him a brass and silver device a little smaller than a mobile phone. Dave had seen one in action earlier. "It does exactly what the name suggests. If any rift begins to form within about a ten-mile radius it will ping. This other one is a communications device." It was about the size of a ballpoint pen. If you see anything suspicious, you press this button, and someone will come to your aid when they're free. If you see a definite incursion, you press it again and the response will be immediate. Don't abuse it."

"I won't. Umm ..." Dave had one more question. "Is this a paid position?"

"Well, I can give you something to cover expenses, but you'll be more effective if you maintain a fairly normal life, a regular job and lifestyle." She handed over half a dozen gold coins. "They're ducats. I think these are worth around £500 each in your time. Don't go splashing this about!" she added on seeing Dave's face break into a grin. "You'll need a nest egg to cover your tracks if people get suspicious. Only sell one at a time."

"Don't worry," Sal said. "I'll keep an eye on him."

"I believe you will."

After that, Sal and Dave left Aspen to get some well-earned sleep. In the morning she was gone, leaving Dave and Sal as the sole guardians against a demonic incursion in the village of Shepherdfordsworth and, they presumed, surrounding parishes.

Dave had some explaining to do when his family saw the state of his eyebrows, but all that was forgotten when he told them that he definitely wasn't moving to a big city because he had found plenty worth staying in Sheppeth for. Later, when he asked if Sal could come for dinner, they all assumed he'd been referring to her. To be fair to them, they were only half wrong.

Stand-To
Alex Morrison

Friday, 30 June 1916, 1:30am

Jack Lamble trudged along the trench, sodden mud sucking at his boots with every painful step. He dreaded what he would find when he took them off – if he ever did.

"Where are the Eighth Devons?" he asked a sentry who leant against the earth wall, raindrops tapping on his helmet. The man tilted his head in the direction Jack had been going. Jack staggered on. He passed men at every zig-zag of the trench. Some shivered on firesteps, gazing into no man's land. Others busied themselves with the night's duties. A few slumped in dugouts, still as corpses. They might have been corpses, for all Jack knew. He shuddered and kept moving.

He had been sent back to battalion HQ – some 800 yards and more than two hours each way across the shattered landscape – with a message, and he would be expected back. The note had almost certainly been a list of dead and wounded. It had been mercifully slim, almost weightless, but heavier lists were coming. Much heavier, he supposed, and littered with names he knew. People he knew. Perhaps, "Private Jack Lamble, Eighth Devons."

He crushed the thought and carried on, going as fast as he could without risking a face-first fall into the suffocating ooze. He passed two men stuck in the slime, with comrades on pallets and duck boards trying to pull them out. As Jack approached another stock-still figure, the glowing tip of a cigarette revealed that this man, at least, was alive.

"Where are the Eighth Devons?" Jack asked.

"We're it."

"Thank God," said Jack.

A deep thud sounded – an artillery shell set loose from the depths of a cold metal barrel.

"God?" said the sentry, as if recalling a half-forgotten school friend. "I'd save your thanks until the morning."

The shell, it turned out, was British – slung across the valley at the German lines near the village of Mametz. A far-off explosion rattled the ground.

"Overshot," said the sentry.

Jack nodded, knowing he was right. As he walked on, he heard two more thuds and blasts, nearer this time. The soaking sky flashed a faint, sickly yellow. Jack glimpsed three faces to his left – including one that stopped him dead.

"Little Jack Lamble?"

The voice jabbed like a hot needle. Jack gripped his rifle strap but said nothing. His mind had somersaulted back across the Channel to a spring day, only a few months earlier, when this face had scorched itself into his memory. He had ducked through the door of the Globe Inn in Frogmore, aching from a day's farm labour. Almost tasting the ale before it touched his lips, he had laughed to find a couple blocking his way, their faces pressed together. But as he tried to step around them, he saw Joy, his fiancée. And he saw Alan Broad.

Now, as if hell's demons took a personal interest in Jack, here stood Broad again: tall, square shouldered, face hard as metal – a man who made Jack look like a boy. Much had happened to Jack since that day in the pub, not least some rudimentary training in how to kill people, but once again he was stunned, wrong-footed – anger and shame bringing his brain to a halt.

"Move along, boy," said Broad.

Jack went, stumbling, unable to find a word or action to cover the hatred boiling in his heart.

* * *

"Stand-to!"

"Stand-to!"

"Stand-to-arms!"

The shout came down the trench in a dozen voices, sergeants of all stripes calling men to duty. With a jolt, Jack realised he had been asleep. To his great relief, the call had come before an NCO – or, worse, some young officer – had spotted him sleeping. He straightened his helmet and felt a hundred pains in every corner of his body. Morning was coming – time for the daily routine of preparing for a pre-dawn attack. But the Germans would not come, Jack knew. The crash of British artillery continued: unseen guns firing unseen shells at unseen Germans. They might even hit a few. Or not. At least the rain has stopped, Jack thought, inhaling what passed for air in the trenches.

Half an hour later, a man brought the rum ration. In another half hour, full daylight had come and the stand-to ended. Jack cleaned his boots, not daring to remove his socks, then hung the boots upside down on sticks poked into the mud, hoping they would dry a little. He did the same with his overcoat. It had rained for a day and a half, and he wanted to use the good weather to full advantage. At seven, he put his boots back on and set off for breakfast.

"That's him," said a voice, as Jack stood in the queue.

Broad was a few places ahead, pointing at Jack as two other men grinned. Jack tensed. As he took his breakfast – weak tea, stale bread and the faintest hint of bacon – he felt the whole trench watching him. He kept his eyes down, an icy prickle of sweat breaking out on his skin. He could fight, but what good would it do? Broad was twice his size, tanned arms like oak branches. Anyway, the artillery had been blasting for days, and no one had been sent out to repair barbed wire at night, so everyone expected a push soon. Maybe Broad would take a bullet. Jack almost smiled at the thought.

Then he was face-down, his breakfast scattered in the mud. Laughter broke out all around. As Jack struggled up, he saw Broad behind him, leering.

"You bastard," Jack growled, and launched himself at Broad.

The fight had barely started when a voice barked, "Stop!" Jack dragged himself back, and looked up to see Broad's fist frozen in mid-air, ready to clang down like a blacksmith's hammer.

"You two," said a scarlet-faced sergeant. "On watch. Six hours. Now."

Two hours later, as most of the Devons tidied the trench, dried their clothes or tried to sleep, Jack and Broad stood in bitter silence, shoulder-to-shoulder on a narrow firestep, rifles aimed through a slit into no man's land. Smoke from the shells and steam from the warming ground drifted aimlessly about, so Jack could barely see beyond bayonet range. Words kept drifting up in his mind, like shapes in murky water, but none escaped.

"Why did you do it?" he said at last, surprising himself.

"What?"

"You know what."

"Take your girl? Because I could. Because she needed a man."

"We were engaged. Doesn't that mean—"

"You weren't *married*."

Huge guns thudded again behind the lines. Explosions tore the ground somewhere in front. Jack wondered if anyone had been unlucky enough to be standing, sitting, kneeling, sleeping right where the shells landed, lives blown out like candle flames. He wondered if some German soldier would carry a list back to HQ, each name to become a letter or telegram or solemn messenger on a doorstep somewhere back in Germany. He wondered which British soldiers might die today, and whether he would carry the list again. Maybe Broad would be on it. The thought gave him a rush of savage joy, like biting into dripping meat cooked on a campfire. A lurch of shame followed on the instant, but he stubbornly held that list in his mind – the list blandly confirming Broad's death.

"You bastard," Jack said, lips twisting as he spat the words.

Broad did not reply. He stood to Jack's right and, both men being right-handed, had his back to Jack as they held their guns at the ready. Jack noticed veins and muscles contract in the big man's neck.

"So you just took her?" Jack persisted.

More shells exploded. Broad said nothing.

"Tell me," Jack said, prodding Broad's shoulder with two fingers.

"Will you shut up, you little rat?" Broad glanced Jack's way then looked along his gun once more.

"No. I'll stick you with a bayonet before I let you ignore—"

An enormous blast shook the world. A shell had fallen short and landed only a hundred yards ahead. Jack flinched. Broad lurched violently, almost dropping his rifle. He recovered himself quickly, forcing the gun back into position as if wrenching it from an invisible grip.

Jack gave a bark of laughter. "Scared, are you? Big man frightened by a little bomb?"

"Shut up," Broad said through clenched teeth.

Shells kept falling as noon passed and the afternoon wore on. Six hours had passed, but no one arrived to relieve them – and Jack wasn't fool enough to leave his post. As the minutes shuffled by, Jack found himself watching Broad. Was he ill? He was certainly sweating, drops leaving lines on his grimy skin. His muscles and veins stood up more than ever, like taut ropes beneath a wind-whipped sail. After another huge blast, Broad started shaking. It was the faintest tremor, which Jack would not have noticed from further away.

They kept to their posts as other men went for tea at six. When the men returned, one brought tea and rock-solid biscuits for Jack and Broad, but no news of when they might stand down. Broad dropped his tea. Jack snorted, and the man who had brought it shrugged and left. Jack had long finished his cup when, "Stand-to!" echoed along the line once more, and the Devons took their posts for dusk.

The Germans did not come.

At last, the angry sergeant came and told Jack and Broad to stand down.

"You're lucky," the sergeant said. "One word out of either of you and I'll put you in no man's land for the night."

They climbed down from the firestep in silence and collapsed on to a pallet that lay at an angle in a partial dugout – the closest thing they would find to a bed. As they tried to rest, the artillery blasted ever harder, shells crashing almost continuously. Broad lay with his arms at his sides, staring up at the deep-blue dusk. Eyes wide, but somehow blank, he seemed to see some horror invisible to Jack. To his surprise, an unwanted flutter of sympathy awoke in Jack.

"You alright?"

Broad said nothing. He just kept staring at the sky.

The artillery raged like punches to the skull all night, and at each call of, "Stand-to!" Jack and Broad took the firestep together. In between, they slumped back to the pallet, enemies side-by-side on duty and at rest.

Jack could see that Broad was shaking in earnest now, teeth chattering despite the mild night. "Cigarette?" he said. A half-box of Woodbines was all he owned, but he wanted to smoke and, despite everything, it seemed wrong not to offer.

"Please," said Broad.

Jack held one out. Broad extended a hand, but its motion was so erratic he would never be able to prise a cigarette from the proffered pack. Seeing this, Jack raised one to the man's mouth. Broad nodded as Jack lit it, then leant back against the boards. They smoked in silence for a minute.

"What happened to you?" Jack said.

Broad took a long drag. "Let's just smoke."

Neither man spoke again until the pre-dawn stand-to. The shelling had stopped. The sun edged uncertainly into clear skies, revealing fine mist in the valley. It could almost have been beautiful, but for the craters – and the knowledge that thousands of men skulked like rats beneath the surface. Barely a sound could be heard. Jack supposed men on both sides suspected what he did: that the time had come.

The anger had drained from him, he realised, to be replaced with something odd: a shape in his chest that did not quite fit. He felt the hot touch of tears, but drew them back at once. Looking along the trench, he saw two officers approaching, sergeants in their wake. At the same moment, a slow breath told him Broad was asleep.

"Wake up, you fool." Jack jabbed him with an elbow.

Broad jerked and turned bloodshot eyes on Jack. "What … ?" Then he saw the officers. When they were gone, he mumbled, "Thanks, Lamble."

Jack nodded. He might feel sorry for the man, but he was no friend.

The rum ration came as the sun climbed. This combined warmth revived Jack's spirits a little. Broad also seemed slightly better. His hand was steady enough to drink.

"Sorry."

At first, Jack was not sure where the sound had come from. Broad's lips had barely moved. "What?"

"I'm sorry." Broad screwed up his eyes as fresh shivers convulsed him.

Jack was about to speak when a series of thuds sounded, followed by a rising drumroll of explosions. Broad pressed his face into the sandbag at the trench-top, eyes shut tight as fists. The fire intensified, the valley before them tossing like an angry sea. Unable to make himself heard, Jack put a hand on Broad's shoulder. A faint tremor shook the larger man. He was crying.

"It's alright," Jack said, but his voice was lost beneath the guns. When the artillery stopped, he knew, the Somme offensive would begin at last. Closing his own eyes, he cleared his heart of the unworthy wish that Broad should die. He hoped the man would live – that he would too – so they could both go home and work out their futures in the green fields of Devon, where they belonged.

A Load of Rubbish
Katie Mallett

Are the British naturally, genetically filthy, I wondered as I picked up another crisp packet, or is this lack of respect for the environment a modern phenomenon? I looked across to the sea, where waves crashed into the rocks at the base of Hillsborough, a promontory that was used by the ancient Dumnonii tribe as a hilltop fortress. In fact Ilfracombe was all hills, built around steep valleys, and many houses were cut into slopes.

We had moved here from the flatlands of Essex after my husband, John, had been made redundant, having decided to use this opportunity to leave the suburban jungle and flee to the open countryside of Devon. The two places were quite different, but there was one thing they had in common – strong wind. Here, it howled round the top of Hillsborough, then tore down the roads, sending wheelie bins careering and sucking recyclables from their crates, often depositing them in the car-parking space that had been cut into our front garden. The terraced house we bought had been built as a holiday home for the Victorian gentry, and I had heard how they would have dreaded visits from the lower classes as they left behind their torn paper and broken bottles to disfigure the coast and countryside. Could it be that these litter louts couldn't help it, any more than seagulls can resist their instinct to tear out food and wrappings from litter bins to strew them all over the promenade?

I don't wonder anymore. I have proof that ordinary people have always discarded unwanted items in the street.

One morning I spotted a new piece of litter in my personal space and went out to put it in my bin, which was already groaning with other people's rubbish including receipts and even gas bills. Fascinated to discover what this new item of detritus might be, I studied it carefully. This was no ordinary piece of twenty-first century junk. It was an invoice, written in beautiful copperplate handwriting and addressed to Mr Ellis, who had apparently bought six white collars and a set of collar studs. It was dated 31 October 1848.

"Where on earth could that have come from?" I asked my husband over dinner. "I mean, it's not your usual sort of litter."

"It's probably from a museum archive," he mumbled through his steak and chips. "Everything gets lost these days: memory sticks, CDs, paper files. Some careless worker took it home and lost it."

"Right. Well I'll keep an eye on the front garden and see if any more turns up."

I didn't have to wait long. A couple of days later I was amazed to find a strangely shaped wine bottle and a very old-fashioned box which apparently had once contained some perfumed soap. Perhaps someone has been digging up a Victorian tip, I thought, though I couldn't fathom out how a glass bottle had blown into my garden. I stored my precious finds in a kitchen cupboard and waited with keen anticipation for something else to turn up. I had thought for a moment about telling someone about this phenomenon, phoning the press or posting on social media, but decided against it. I didn't want a crowd of ghost-hunting geeks gathering in front of our house..

Every day I went out to do my clean up, but nothing else unusual arrived until one Monday morning, about week after my first discovery. I almost tripped up over something just below my bottom step. It was a very rusty flat iron. That definitely didn't blow in from anywhere. I decided then and there to sit up at night, to try to see where the rubbish was coming from.

"I have to do it, John," I explained, countering my husband's protestations. "How else can I find out?"

"Well, I'll sit up with you," he said, "... for a while, anyway."

He had to go to work the following day so it would have been impossible for him to sit up all night but I was impatient to find out what was going on. I persuaded him to sit with me by the lounge window, watching and waiting. He lasted until two o'clock before sloping off to crawl into bed, but I kept up my vigil. There was nothing. I slept through the afternoon, and decided to sit up the following night. John wouldn't do it again, and I didn't blame him. I took my seat by the window and waited, resisting the urge to shut my eyes. Once again, there was nothing to see. Just one more try tomorrow night, I thought, and then I'll give up for now.

By then I was feeling very tired, and rather fractious. John was becoming really annoyed with me and we had a monstrous row before he stomped off to bed at eleven o'clock. I took up my usual position by the lounge window and turned the lights off. I'd gathered together a couple of bottles of water and some biscuits to help me through the long dark hours and put the radio on to stop me going to sleep. Speech would be better than music, I decided, so I tuned in to Radio 4 and started listening to a programme about someone's travels in China. The programme finished, the shipping forecast came on, and then the World Service.

It was about three o'clock when I noticed something weird. There was a light in the front garden, but it didn't seem to be attached to anything, or anyone. At first it was dim, then it brightened into a startling flash, like an old-fashioned camera bulb going off. When my eyes had recovered from the flash I peered out of the window and could just make out something lying on the ground. Although afraid of what might be out there, I couldn't wait until the morning to see what it was, so opened the front door quietly and tiptoed down the steps. There on the ground was a broken fan. It had been a good fan, from the look of it. Fine lace stretched between the ivory ribs, which were decorated with carvings of birds and flowers. I took it indoors, vowing to be brave enough to discover what had caused the light.

I explained my plan to John late the next evening. He thought I was mad.

"Sit out on the front steps in the middle of the night? What on earth will the neighbours think? I don't know what I think, even. Perhaps you ought to be locked up."

"Oh, you're not curious then?" I retorted. "I would have thought you'd like to know what's going on in our patch."

"Well, you find out; I'm going to bed," he replied testily. "Take something with you to defend yourself, though, in case some nutter comes by."

He clearly thought that the light I saw was a figment of my imagination, and that the fan had arrived by some mundane means.

Risking certification and pneumonia I went out at midnight and sat on the front steps. A couple of drunks staggered by. Thankfully they didn't see me as I shrank into the shadows. An owl flew silently overhead. I was alarmed by a rat running out from behind the wheelie bins in the garden opposite. Nothing else stirred. Lights went out in the homes all around me and the world grew quiet. I could feel my heavy head nodding forwards as I fought the urge to retreat to my cosy bed ...

But there it was: a dim light just in front of me. It glowed and brightened to a halo, then a shaft, of brilliant white – and it seemed to be pulling me in. I felt myself drawn to the centre of the light source like iron filings to a magnet and for a second all was blinding chaos.

I landed on my knees in a muddy street, smeared with horse manure and slime. When I looked up I saw no houses, but fields rolling down to a small harbour filled with sailing boats.

As I raised my head further I caught sight of a bearded man standing in front of me. He could have featured as a villain in a Dickens novel, garbed as he was in ragged clothing, dishevelled and dirty. As he lurched towards me there was the unmistakable stink of stale gin. He swayed side to side for a moment, then raised his right hand. I realised he was wielding a knife. I felt it hit me then pierce the front of my shoulder. I could feel blood running down my arm. The man lifted his hand with the knife again but, as he did so, I felt myself being dragged back through the tunnel of light.

I landed with a thud on the ground below the bottom step in my front garden; beside me lay a bloodstained knife. Wincing with pain from my shoulder, and breathless with shock, I picked up the knife and dragged myself up the steps to my front door and in to safety. Examining myself in the hallway mirror, I saw a tear in my jacket. I quickly took if off, ripped off my blouse and looked at my shoulder. There was a stain of something dark red down my arm, but no fresh blood. There was no open wound but a ragged scar – a scar I'd never seen before. The blood on the knife was dry.

I didn't wake John then, but in the morning I told him what had happened. He was as puzzled as me, but forbade me to do any more night vigils.

"You'd better get a tetanus injection, just in case," he suggested. "Though what a doctor will make of a century-old wound I wouldn't like to say." Then he added, "Are you sure you didn't do that yourself? Perhaps you fell over in the garden and landed on something sharp, and forgot about it."

"John, clearly this was no scratch," I said. "How could I forget about it?"

He shrugged, and left for work. Something changed between us then. He didn't believe me and clearly didn't trust me anymore. Every day I had to account for my actions. I could see him looking at my arms and legs as if expecting to see some evidence of self-harm.

I made an appointment with our clinic nurse and had the injection, as a precaution, my cover story a garden makeover with its attendant risks. I didn't even see the doctor. There seemed little point. I could imagine him laughing as I explained where the scar had come from.

Since then I've tried to find out what happened in my front garden in Victorian times. It seems it was by a well-used lane out of the town where a milestone was a meeting point for villains, traders and lovers. No doubt all kinds of rubbish ended up on the ground. Why it should find its way through time to my garden is still a mystery.

Nothing has arrived since my adventure. John says I should bury the stuff and forget about it. I might, if it weren't for the lingering stiffness and pain in my shoulder. I can't help sitting up some nights to see if anything happens, though I stay indoors out of harm's way. You might think this is a load of rubbish, but I've got the scars, mental and physical, to prove it.

As for those Dumnonii up on Hillsborough, I dread to think what they threw on the ground, but I don't intend trying to find out. I've had enough rubbish for one lifetime and if anyone asks about the scar I tell them I fell over in the garden. The rest is just history.

Raparee Beach
Caroline Berry

The moon was high and round, the night was calm and even the gulls were quiet, settled happily in their nests. Gwen couldn't sleep; the moonlight kept sneaking between the curtains and it was too quiet without the gulls' usual restless night-time bickering.

Kicking aside the duvet, Gwen gave up on sleep, roused Milly, her 'Heinz 57' dog, and headed out for their favourite walk to Raparee beach. She loved Raparee: not only was it a lovely place to be, but it had a fascinating, if rather grisly, history. Gwen had learned all about it, as a member of the Friends of Raparee.

Descending the steps onto the beach, Gwen thought it looked like a watercolour painting with the washed-out silvery-blue sand and shingle. Milly ran around sniffing the rocks and digging holes, enjoying the unexpected bonus walk. Gwen wandered down to the sea, her footsteps crunching as if she was walking in snow. The sea was completely flat with only the gentle breaking of small white lines revealing where the waves met the sand. She gazed absent-mindedly across the horizon, vaguely taking in the lights glistening at the harbour, the reflection of the moon shimmering on the ocean's surface and the stillness in the air. Milly's deep bark roused her from her reverie. She turned to see what had disturbed the dog and froze. Her breath caught in her throat. Milly ran to her and leant on her leg, the warm body surprisingly comforting, despite the fact that it was shaking.

There, emerging from the rocks, the sand and, behind her, from the sea, were hundreds of luminous figures. They slowly shuffled towards Gwen in a strange lurching motion. Gwen glanced downwards; every single one of them had fettered feet restricting their movement. No footprints were left on the sand, no drag marks were made by the chains. As they approached, they reached out, revealing shackled hands. Glassy pale eyes stared beseechingly towards Gwen and horror took over her fear as she saw the heavy manacles tightly enclosing their translucent wrists; they must have caused so much pain when these people were alive.

The apparitions were gaunt, with hollow-cheeked faces. There were men, women, and even children. They encircled Gwen and Milly, their sunken eyes pleading silently. Petrified, Gwen could feel tears running down her cheeks.

"I'm sorry," she whispered. "I don't know what you want …"

She fell to her knees on the damp sand as they closed in around her, dropping her head into her hands.

"Please … please … I don't know what to do."

A cold breeze caressed Gwen's cheek and she looked up. The ghosts were gone – except for the spectre of a small girl in rags with tight curls framing her features. Gwen didn't feel afraid of this little girl and noticed that Milly had stopped shaking. The girl reached her cuffed hands to Gwen, who took one. It felt odd, like holding a damp sponge: if she pressed too tightly her fingers would pass through and connect with her thumb.

The little girl led her up the steep steps towards Hillsborough, Milly close at their heels. At the curve of the steps the little girl dropped Gwen's hand and stepped off the path into the shrubbery there, gesturing towards the tangled, wild patch of land in front of them.

Gwen was confused. "I don't know what you're trying to tell me."

The little girl, her features solemn and hands crossed over her chest, turned to face Gwen, who watched, rooted to the spot, as the child sank backwards into a horizontal position before disappearing down into the gorse and the ground beneath. She barely had time to take a breath before the little girl reappeared by her side, staring with her pearly eyes; she was clearly trying to communicate something – but what? Pointing to the ground again, urgently now, the child clapped her hands in encouragement as Milly dashed forward, scenting. The dog, homing in on one spot, started digging excitedly amongst the twisted roots, while the little girl jumped with excitement.

Gwen's mouth dropped open as realisation finally struck. "Is this your grave?"

The little girl nodded.

"Are the others from the beach buried here too?"

The little girl smiled as she nodded her affirmation.

"But why? Why are you buried here?"

The little girl frowned and shook her chained hands, holding them out to Gwen, who reached out and enclosed them in her own. The little girl closed her eyes and Gwen did the same as her stomach jolted like a lift in freefall …

* * *

When Gwen opened her eyes, she was still holding the little girl's hand but the surroundings were different; the weather was different. In place of the still, calm night was howling wind and rain. She turned and saw, as if through a veil, the figures of five men, wearing very old-fashioned clothes, digging where Milly had been digging just a moment ago. But Milly was no longer there. One of the men spoke, his voice muffled and warped by the strange barrier between them.

"Quick! We must bury these bodies so they don't know."

Gwen stared in disbelief: she was watching the excavation of a huge burial pit. The twisted bodies of men, women, and children, chained together, lay heaped at the edge of the hole. Gwen thought she recognised a face in the pile and, as it was hidden by the arm of another body sliding over it, she shuddered and looked down – only to see the same little face staring up at her.

Gwen knew from the Friends of Raparee group that a famous eighteenth-century shipwreck only recorded forty deaths, but that there were thought to be more. She also knew there were rumours that the captain refused to be guided into the harbour because he had prisoners of war onboard that he planned to sell as slaves. But this was worse.

"Were you a slave?" Gwen asked the girl, who first shook her head, then nodded.

"Were you captured to be sold as slaves?"

The little girl nodded sadly.

"How many of you were there?"

The little girl shrugged; Gwen realised that, as a female child in the eighteenth century, she would probably not have been taught to count.

"There were about fifty ghosts on the beach, were they all going to be sold as slaves like you?"

The little girl nodded.

"Were the prisoners of war going to be sold as slaves?"

The little girl nodded.

Gwen sighed.

"This is terrible." She paused. "Is that why you and the others are still here?"

The little girl nodded. Gwen stared at the gruesome scene from the past.

"This is awful. I don't want to see any more."

The little girl took Gwen's hand and the scene before them faded. They were back to the calm moonlit night with Milly ahead of them flicking out soil from a large hole. Gwen called her and the dog happily ran back to them. The little girl smiled and patted Milly's head.

Gwen knelt down so she was face to face with the little girl.

"I promise you now, that I will make sure you are all freed from your chains and this hidden mass grave. The truth will be known at last."

The little girl gave Gwen a big smile – then faded from view.

Gwen got onto her knees and dug with her hands where Milly had started digging. To tell the others, to tell the world, she needed proof. She would say Milly had started acting strangely and became obsessed with that area and she decided to investigate. Soon her sore, dirtied hands hit something hard. She scraped at the soil and revealed part of a manacle. She knew if she dug further she would find bones. Gwen's face hardened with determination. She was going to keep her promise; she would contact the press; she would get the truth known. Calling to Milly, she headed home.

* * *

High on the hill above, the ghosts looked down as their mortal remains were treated with a respect they had not been shown in life; their ethereal manacles vanished, twisted bodies became straight, their once-contorted faces now looked as they had in life, before they had been stolen from their homes.

Their eyes turned heavenwards and their ghostly forms disintegrated into millions of specks of light, fireflies dancing in the wind, spiralling into the sky.

The Final Battle
Val Allsup

The sky darkened as the clouds rolled in and the waves grew stronger now the tide had finally turned. The sea frothed and splashed as it washed up to the dark stones of the quay. The rising water began to cover the muddy expanse of the estuary, profoundly changing the landscape.

As he drew his coat tighter round him, Captain Tim watched the gusting wind pull at the marsh grass by the shore. Every intake of breath brought with it the mingled smells of salt and smoke. Pulling his hat down and his collar up, he turned to the remaining crew – just six left now – huddled together in the hull. So many had already gone, leaving this motley crew as the sole defenders of the ship. He had started low in the ranks but now the others respected and were happy to follow his leadership.

As they shared their last few scraps of food he talked them through his plan. He thought the enemy would make one last attempt to break through before the hour became too late and the weather too inclement. They needed to brace themselves and be prepared to defend their ship for as long as necessary. "Get the cannons ready!" he instructed firmly. "Arm yourselves and keep vigilant; we don't know where they'll strike first!."

The youngest member of the crew was placed on watch. He was a recent recruit but had already impressed the others with his tenacity and bravery. The rest of the crew made thorough checks and practiced their drills. They took stock of the armoury and shared out the munitions between them. They were ready.

A few tense minutes followed where the silence was only broken by the buffeting winds and the cries of curious seagulls wheeling overhead. Suddenly, the young lookout shouted a warning: the enemy were approaching. A wall of noise hit Captain Tim as a group of enemy fighters emerged from the shadows, hollering and bellowing as they advanced. The air was thick with missiles whistling overhead. Tim ducked as he shouted commands to the crew, but his voice was soon drowned out by loud bangs as a few of the missiles made contact with the ship. He used his hands instead to marshal his crew and on his signal they started fighting back. Cannon shots were fired and yells of celebration followed as they found their mark. They started firing in earnest, striving to protect their vessel.

But then disaster struck: an enemy fighter had managed to board the ship. Captain Tim rushed to meet him and grabbed the intruder before he could attack anyone. He wasn't experienced in hand-to-hand combat but he managed to get the upper hand and pushed his adversary back over the side. He turned and saw another intruder climbing up pointing a weapon at a young crew-mate. Tim didn't hesitate before he bravely took a running jump to block the enemy's shot. He saw it all happen in slow motion; he had mistimed the jump and slid past before the shot was fired. He groaned as he landed and turned round expecting to see the worst but, fortunately, he had distracted the shooter enough to throw off his aim and the young crewman was unscathed. They realised their lucky escape and both ran to grab the intruder and bundle him off the ship before he had the chance to re-load and take another shot.

This seemed to mark a turning point in the battle, as Captain Tim and his crew now went from strength to strength. They were more accurate with their shots and their determination to win drove the attackers back. They soon heard the opponents' chief yelling, "Retreat!" and, "Fall back!" and were elated as they watched the enemy scurry away dejectedly.

Captain Tim's crew cheered wildly as they celebrated their survival, against the odds, in this final skirmish of the day. Tim smiled as he surveyed the battleground; it had been a long day of fighting but he was delighted with this final victory, won under his command.

A loud shout broke through Tim's reverie and he turned to see his mum waving across the large grassy expanse of the playground. In the blink of an eye the vista turned from the ravaged, war-torn landscape of his imagination to the pleasant surroundings of Fremington Quay, albeit on a cloudy, squally day. The battleship became, once more, the wooden pirate ship of the playground; the smell of a smoky barbecue braving the wind reclaimed its innocence; the fighters were a mix of tourists and local children all under the age of ten, with Tim's rank a compliment to his leadership but with no military founding; and the pretend sounds of toy guns, grenades and cannons made by the children themselves were now replaced with squeals of joy as ice creams were handed out to friend and foe alike, the allegiances of the game forgotten. New friendships made from the camaraderie of playground warfare were toasted with their cones – never too cold or windy for an ice cream in Devon!

The parents listened to vivid descriptions of battles won and lost, each child clamouring to describe their part in the adventures. As she listened, Tim's mum smiled to hear their tales of bravado and derring-do, remembering the imaginary battles of her own childhood. But, as the wind whipped along the quay, she gripped her coat tighter round her, hoping these children would never have to battle in a real war. These might be the last days of this year's summer but she hoped that the world leaders would not cause this to be an end to the summer of their lives.

Scone With the Wind
Jade Ruby

Almost hidden from view amongst Devon's tumbling hills, the tiny hamlet was straight out of a storybook with its chocolate-box surroundings. A criss-cross tapestry of green pastures, ancient trees and vibrant meadows lay beyond, intersected by the two tributaries that joined here to give the village its name. The Dingle and Dell passed underneath an old stone bridge before gaining momentum, widening into a sleek body of water as it descended through the valley in pursuit of the River Taw.

Framing the double-arched bridge was the smattering of woodland that became awash with bluebells in late spring. This is where the children of the village had always played, collecting fistfuls of wildflowers for their mothers, throwing sticks into the water and extracting themselves from the trees when it was time to go home for supper.

Sadly, the number of children had dwindled over the years as families moved towards Barnstaple and Ilfracombe. Most of the residents of Dingley Dell were now embracing their eighth decade in style, but there were exceptions to this rule. Some of the ladies of the village had swapped the simple pleasures of crafting and casual gossip for a hard-line of competitive ailments, curtain twitching and heated rumour spreading. Referred to as the 'Dillydallies', they believed the nickname was a term of endearment and were blind to the eye-rolls it triggered.

Dillydally members cast a shadow over the lively social scene, oppressing the twice-weekly coffee mornings, bingo and other events in the church hall. They held centre stage when the manor house hosted celebrations, and they took umbrage if occasions didn't factor in a seat for their discerning rears. Funerals were their favourite pastime, and many a grieving child or widow had come a cropper when they didn't request their attendance at private services.

However, there was one event that absolutely everyone looked forward to each year, and that was the Great Show. It was the highlight of the calendar, the word on everyone's lips and something that positively thrilled the Dillydallies. The Great Show was cliché: overwhelmingly, quintessentially English, and a golden opportunity to sample a slice of traditional Devon life. Or, at least it had been, once upon a time. Now it seemed to be more of an occasion for showing off.

Every May, striped bunting would appear and each front lawn would be coiffed to perfection, not a hedge out of place and all blooms standing to attention. Tents would be erected in all their white-as-a-sheet glory on the village green, the grass underneath smelling damp and earthy from the morning dew. The tables would be wiped down to sparkling perfection and dressed with gingham cloths ready to be adorned with antiques, collectables and other treasures.

Stalls favoured by the Dillydallies tended to be bric-a-brac and other paraphernalia often unfairly associated with ladies of advancing age, such as fancy doilies, small ceramic animals and fine china figures. These attractions held a morbid appeal. Following the inevitable passing of a neighbour, you could guarantee their beloved items would end up on the selling tables to be pawed at.

Of course, the pièce de résistance was the baking competition, a flamboyant affair where coveted prizes were given out for the best creations. This is what generated so much fervour – the Dillydallies lived for this annual showering of confectionary. It had become a rite of passage, a chance for the ten-strong clutch of ladies and one token gent to produce their yearly offerings.

Indulgently, the roster of themes was repeated every six years or so, rewarding the body of judges (also members of the Dillydallies despite the bias) with the same treats they'd taste-tested for years. There was an unspoken agreement that the oldest member would win gold, and a pecking order was established for silver and bronze. A conciliatory prize would be offered to one lucky villager just as an incentive to take part.

Lavender Forbury had been the recipient of the gold for around five years running due to the fact that she was an impressive ninety-two years young. The judges gushed with false compliments, enthusing about her dry drizzle cakes, tasteless tarts and stale scones while she beamed behind her enormous spectacles. In truth, her pies were painfully plain and her sausage rolls were, for want of a better term, utterly revolting. Once this charade was over for another year, the competitors could rest at night knowing full well that their humble silvers and bronzes were the real winners.

This year, things were due to change. The three judges were no more, one undergoing an operation, one thrust into the care of her daughter following a bad fall, and the other, a formidable character, was now six feet under. The Dillydallies were wheezing at the thought of her worldly goods being on display on the bric-a-brac stall.

Clarice Blunt was most concerned about the new judging regime. It had been her turn to win silver for her trusty rock cakes as per schedule.

"Scones again," she grumbled on judgement day. "It isn't fair; the rules have been in place for years!"

"Ridiculous," Ada Muggins, agreed - mainly because she had been promised bronze.

"Not just any scones, but 'jazzed up' scones! What's wrong with nice sultanas?" Clarice scowled.

"Tradition is key." Ada shook her chins, the first and last wobbling a fraction after the other, creating an effect not dissimilar to a Newton's Cradle. "I understand a nice plain scone if appetite prevails, or perhaps even a dash of lemon curd."

"Submitting them all the night before too – they won't be fresh!" Clarice intoned. "Don't get me started on the change of venue. What is this?"

She gestured at the grand hall, condemning the ornate ceiling and lavish walls of the manor as if batting away a fly.

"We didn't need to move indoors; the tents were adequate." Ada ignored the fevered gale blowing outside. "You did well getting here before everyone else to check they hadn't spoiled."

"To think I got told off for it!" Clarice fumed. "I was only adjusting the plates, how dare they accuse me of meddling."

Her outrage caused her hip to jolt the table, plates of scones jittering almost in anticipation as the new judge made her way down the table. She was a strong, rounded woman in her mid-fifties, resplendent in a red woollen dress and long, dark hair.

"Violet Pledger is mutton dressed as lamb," Ada scoffed. "Her poor mother would be aghast."

She glowered as the new Lady of the Manor and now sole judge approached their end of the table. Ada was feeling particularly wounded, having enjoyed much influence before Violet took over. She'd spent a lot of time at the manor.

"Very unusual flavours – but I really like the cheese." Violet encouraged a misty-eyed baker. "Quite memorable."

She made a note and addressed Clarice and Ada with a prim nod.

"Ah, are these sultanas or something a little more exciting? Pecans?" She prodded one of Ada's creations hopefully.

"Heavens no!" Ada regarded her crossly and quickly adopted a forlorn expression.

Violet didn't say anything more, but her disappointment was obvious. She had barely swallowed Clarice's offering before she moved on to the next competitor. Young and fresh in a flowery dress, Mabel Pledger was Violet's daughter and a new challenger for the baking crown.

"O-ho!" Ada quavered in voyeuristic glee. "Disqualified I imagine, right Violet?" She winked at the judge, suddenly adopting a conspiratorial manner.

"Whatever do you mean, Ada?" Violet barely broke her stride. "Mabel has baked the scones, sourced the cream and made the jam herself." She chewed thoughtfully. "Delicious." She smiled at the young woman, who blushed prettily.

"She put the jam on first!" Ada was incredulous. "We're in Devon!"

"It's hardly sacrilege." Violet was unmoved despite the gasps from the assembled onlookers.

"It's not jam," Mabel proffered, her voice trembling slightly. "It's raspberry and gin compote. Also, the cream has a touch of elderflower."

"I really detect that coming through." Violet had eaten half the scone and was starting on the remainder.

"It's cheating if it's your daughter," Ada grumbled.

Violet's eyes flashed.

"I think it's cheating if it's the same winner every year, don't you?" she admonished, causing Ada to clutch at her ample bosom as if scalded.

Lavender was next, balancing delicately on her walking frame.

"I know the recipe asked for eight, but I'm in my nineties dear," she appealed with large, glistening eyes. "I could only manage six, what with my arthritis."

"Goodness." Violet handled them carefully. "They are very ... symmetrical. Almost identical."

She took a bite, the assembled crowd gathered around her.

"Hmm, I can taste something a little bitter ... Preservatives," she remarked, discreetly spitting the mouthful onto a handkerchief. She regarded Lavender carefully. "They taste almost like Farmhouse Pride: the very same scones I grew up with, that can still be bought at the village shop. In fact, if you turn it over, you can usually see the mark at the bottom."

Sure enough, turning over the scone revealed a faint 'F'. The crowd gasped again.

"Well, what can you expect? I'm in my nineties!" Lavender snapped, unrepentant but clearly shaken.

"Disqualified!" Violet declared brazenly. She swept onto the next plate.

"The nerve!" Clarice cried, consoling furious Lavender. "To upset an old lady so."

The awards ceremony was a bitter pill to swallow for the Dillydallies. There wasn't a flash of gold, silver or bronze between them. To add insult to injury, Clarice had been awarded the consolation prize for effort.

"She didn't even bother to give me the award herself," she sniffed a few days later.

"I heard she had taken ill," Ada gloated. "Food poisoning, probably from her daughter's scones. Elderflower cream indeed," she snorted.

"Poor Violet." Clarice tried to fold her gnarled face into a sorrowful expression. "I knew she should have stuck with tradition."

Geraldine, another particularly venomous lady, was propped up against the fence for a good debrief. "Ah," she shook her head, "but it wasn't food poisoning! She's a very poorly lady. They think it was deliberate."

"Deliberate?" Ada enquired.

"Word is they found a high level of warfarin in her system." Geraldine's eyes shone with the excitement of imparting knowledge. "She's got some sort of condition; the levels were enough to give her a heart attack."

"Poor woman. To think, her own daughter …"

"Police have ruled her out because she didn't make the scones: she arrived back from university just before the judging."

"What!" Ada exclaimed. "Then who made them?"

"Violet herself." Whispered Geraldine. "Apparently she did it to teach us old ladies a lesson! Well, look what that's done. More fool her. Of course, she wouldn't have poisoned herself, so the police are checking the CCTV. Violet had it installed in the manor after finding all her mother's silverware gone."

Clarice abruptly turned away from the gate, wringing her hands as she stepped into the cottage. She hesitated by the sink, fingers gripping the porcelain.

"Clarice?" her husband called. "Clarice?"

"Yes?" she barked, her voice shrill.

"Have you seen my tablets?"

"Tablets?"

"Yes, my warfarin? I bloody mixed them up and put them in with the laxatives. I've certainly had a clear out. I'll be writing to complain to the pharmacy; why do all the packets always look the same?"

His tall frame joined her by the window, surveying the street with interest. "Geraldine's looking well," he commented approvingly.

"Oh hello, look, there's Percival's grandson." He peered through the net curtains. "Is that what they're driving these days? Flashy business, being a policeman."

He didn't notice Clarice rapidly turning different shades of green and grey.

"Seems like he's heading this way. Get the kettle on, dear, call me old fashioned, but it's tradition to offer a gentleman of the constabulary a nice brew."

He strode to the door, reaching for the plate of scones on the counter.

"Ah, young Percy Jnr," he said in greeting. "Come in! You must try one of our Clarice's scones. They won the consolation prize in the Great Show, don't you know!"

Home Is Where the Heart Is
Maria Kinnersley

"You did what?" Her voice rose as each word shot out of her tight-lipped mouth.

"Jeannie my love, I put in an offer for the bungalow. It was too good a chance to miss." He paused, then murmured, "And we did say this move would be my choice."

She threw her bag onto the bed. It bounced off and landed on the carpet, the contents strewn over the floor.

She gave a muttered curse. "But we've already made an offer on the other place," she said. "You know I fell in love with it. I've always dreamt about a house like that."

He sat on the bed and patted the space beside him. She hesitated, then slowly sank onto the mattress, her back rigid. He put his arm around her shoulders. She shrugged it off.

"All I'm saying is that I feel this place is more for us. We can make this one our own."

She stared straight ahead, immobile.

"Anyway, it was a silly offer," he continued. "They probably won't accept it."

Jeannie thought back to the last few frantic months.

This had all started during a camping holiday in Devon. They'd met a few people on the same site, who all seemed to be following their dreams. A couple were travelling the country for six months in their mobile home. Another pair had sold up and moved to the other end of the country to start anew. As she watched Paul, she saw he was inspired. Hell, she thought, even she was.

On the last evening, they sat outside their tent, each with a glass of wine. Paul, she noticed, seemed lost in his thoughts.

"Let's have an adventure," he said finally, breaking the companionable silence. "Let's sell up and move down here; have a completely new life. We've been saying how bored we are. The kids hardly ever visit. We can't just wait for them to turn up."

"It does sound a great idea," she said. "But are you sure? After all, you've spent all your life in the southeast."

"I've never been more certain," he said, his gaze steady. "I can't wait to get started."

It hadn't been straightforward. Their property hadn't sold and the bungalow they had set their hearts on in Buckfastleigh was sold to a higher bidder.

They had all but given up hope when, the week before Christmas, a couple made an offer. The only snag was that they had to be out by the end of March.

"So," Paul grumbled. "We now have to rush around like idiots after Christmas, when we already know that there is nothing available. Maybe it's not meant to be."

While he went out for a walk, Jeannie researched what was available on the various estate agent's websites.

"Nothing near Buckfastleigh," she murmured.

She stared at the screen, head cocked to one side. "Hmm … What if I widened the search?"

Her fingers rattled over the keys, then she contemplated the new list, for a village called Liverton, now before her. "Ah, this is more like it."

She printed out the various properties she found and put the pages on the table for Paul to view on his return. The expression on his face changed from po-faced to excited as he flipped over the pages.

"Jeannie, you're a genius. Let's sort out some viewings for after Christmas."

As they travelled from their small hotel to their first viewing, they appeared to be surrounded by rainbows.

"This is a rainbow county," Paul said. "Maybe it's a sign. See how close the ends of the rainbows are to our car?"

So it was with an air of anticipation that they arrived at their first potential property. Jeannie fell in love with it from the off. An executive-style home with four bedrooms.

"Such a lovely staircase," she raved. "The extra bedroom would make a great study."

"A staircase does not make a home," Paul retorted. "I'd like to have another look in the afternoon. I have a feeling it could be dark when the sun has gone from the rear. And every room needs work."

"We've other properties to see. We don't need to make a firm decision yet," she said.

She hoped that the others she had selected would not be as wonderful as this one.

And the other homes were indeed not ideal until they drew up to the last property. The front garden was unkempt, filled with overgrown shrubs, and the bungalow was plain. This wouldn't do at all, she thought happily. Then, her heart sank as she heard Paul's next words.

"Now, this is more like it."

He jumped out of the car and strode up the path, eager to get a closer look. She followed after him at a much slower pace, her heart plunging ever lower.

"Give it a chance," he murmured as he noticed her glum expression. "You don't know what it's like inside."

She gave a nod as the door opened.

As soon as he had walked in, he broke his own rule of remaining impassive while viewing and enthused.

"Oh, yes, this is just right. Look, love, the hall's spacious. What a lovely layout. Oh yes, I like this," as he explored the roomy bedrooms.

She, on the other hand, found all the faults. "Paul, love," she said. "It's all-electric. There's no central heating, no gas, the conservatory roof is—"

"Oh, it's nothing that can't be sorted," he declared as he glanced at the garden.

After, as they talked to the estate agent outside, Jeannie realised the depth of Paul's feelings for this property.

"It's a lovely place," Paul said. "It reminds me of my Mum and Dad's property …" His voice was choked and he walked away, leaving the estate agent and Jeannine gazing at each other, perplexed.

And now she had discovered that he had made an offer without discussing it.

The following day was their last. They'd already decided they were going to have a walk around the area. Paul had given up trying to discuss his choice of property. She clammed up whenever he mentioned it. Even this walk was not ideal. He had reached for her hand in a quiet country lane but she snatched it away, refusing all contact.

She strode around a bend, nearly knocking into someone.

"Oh, I'm so sorry," she said. "I didn't see you."

The figure swayed a little then righted herself.

"It's okay. No damage done. In a hurry, were you?"

Jeannie examined the woman in front of her: about half her size, with a brown wrinkled face and a curly wood walking stick firmly gripped in one hand. Jeannie wondered for a moment whether this was a piskie.

Paul, catching up with Jeannie, answered for her, "Not in a hurry at all; in fact we're hoping to move down here. We're just exploring the area."

"I'm Rosie," the woman said. "Come and see my house. It's not far."

The three of them strolled up the quiet lane towards a large cottage. It was perfect. There were even roses around the front door. Rosie walked forward and opened the gate.

"Come in. Have a nosy round my lovely garden."

As they wandered around, Paul saw that Jeannie was captivated by the place. Rosie watched her.

"It wasn't always like this, you know," she said. "When we married and moved in here, it was run down. The garden was a wilderness." She leant on her stick, her eyes seeming to view the past. "But Ron, my husband, worked hard on the house and got it shipshape." Her voice faded and became quiet.

"It's beautiful now," said Jeannie with a gentle smile. "The garden is glorious."

"Ah, well, it's full of memories. You see that rose bush there? That's in remembrance of my son, who died twenty years ago." She sighed. "Everything in this house and garden has a reason to be here. We worked hard to make it our home. And now, with Ron gone, this is where I'm happiest."

As they made their way back to their hotel, Paul's mobile gave a buzz. He viewed it.

"It's a text message from the estate agent. They've accepted my offer."

Jeannie moved to a field gate and leant on it as she watched the sheep there. She was silent.

"We don't have to move, love," he murmured, as he moved forward and held her hand. She gripped it hard.

"No," she whispered. "I see it now." Her eyes were shining, and Paul saw her tears through her smile. "We can make that bungalow our home. Put our stamp on it if you like. And," – her voice wobbled – "we can make it a place of memories."

Dolores Goes Camping
Jade Ruby

Dolores is a Drag Queen and fabulous is she,
She's glamorous and striking and fills the crowd with glee.
Alas she has a weak point, and it really is a pain,
Her vanity is plentiful, her patience but a grain.
The audience adores her, but her cup is never full,
Backstage she rants and raves like a fearsome raging bull.

One day, tired of all her gripes and all her worldly woes,
I said, "Who cares, Dolores, for the sequins on your clothes?
Your shoes are just as fine without boasting well-known names,
And your wigs are far superior to all the other dames'."
I said she was ridiculous and full of airs and graces,
She claimed she really wasn't, and pulled some silly faces.

"Okay," said I, "then prove that you have got some inner grit:
Borrow all my camping gear and show me you can rough it.
My favourite place to holiday is North Devon, near the coast,
I reckon if you tried it you'd last a day at most."
"That's easy!" roared Dolores, puffing up her chest with vigour,
"I can do that with my eyes closed." I couldn't help but snigger.

"Hurrah!" I said, "That's excellent; let's take it up a notch,
Take along your heels, your skirts and all that old hotchpotch.
The challenge is to spend a week donning all your gear,
From the make-up on your face to the pads upon your rear.
Devon won't have seen a Queen in all her fire and fury,
Have you got what it takes to sway the ladies of the jury?"

Now Dolores is no quitter so she didn't shy away,
Instead she said, "You're on, my friend, let's do this: I will play."
Four enormous suitcases she stuffed with all her might,
With shiny things and bodysuits – and twenty pairs of tights.
Her Fiat huffed and puffed as she squeezed inside the door,
I slammed it shut and waved as she made off to explore.

Several long hours later – several service station bogs,
She made it past the border; it was raining cats and dogs.
She'd surely freeze her pants off: it was Devon's wildest weather,
And if I know Dolores, this thought ruffled all her feathers.
But she focused on finding a little patch of heaven,
In the glorious green countryside of beautiful North Devon.

She pitched her tent at Barricane, it really was a treat,
A gorgeous beach and café with delicious things to eat.
"Oh how lovely!" cried Dolores, looking at her tent with pride,
The spot seemed quite idyllic – when the beach was at low tide.
Regrettably Dolores was in a tearing hurry,
To get inside the beach café and tuck into a curry.

Evening came – she fell asleep, she really was quite weary,
But her size nine feet were sticking out the tent flaps, very clearly.
Full of curry, sound asleep, she missed the surfers leaping,
She also missed the tide change and the sea slowly in-creeping.
Her snores rang out across the beach, just like a power saw,
A wave came up and caught her shoes and took them from shore.

Dolores woke up with a start and screamed out for her shoes,
"Give them back you fiend; those were my favourite Jimmy Choos!"
The sea retreated smugly, its billows swelled with pride,
Leaving poor Dolores seething; she vowed to tan its hide.
But of course, to no avail: no-one can fight the sea,
Against the rising tide she had to pack her things and flee.

Not taking any chances she retreated to the car,
She really wasn't risking it when she had come so far.
Unfortunately for Dolores she hadn't yet been told,
That a gang of local seagulls had really grown quite bold.
Squabbling and barging, they flew down on treacherous wings,
They somehow got the boot ajar and made off with her things.

She woke up with a start and, longing for some bacon,
She looked round for the cool box and thought herself mistaken;
A bright pink frilly flag flew from the mirror of her car,
'Oh no,' she thought, 'That's not a flag, it's a massive lacy bra!'
Horrified, she realised as it fluttered in the breeze,
That bra was hers, and what were those? Her knickers the trees.

Several hours later she had shaken off her gloom,
Mainly as she'd cheated and booked herself a room.
She'd found a charming little pub at Lynmouth's pretty heart,
A delightful place for stuffing ones face and admiring local art.
High above was Lynton and breathtaking views of the bay,
'Too far to walk,' Dolores thought, so she took the cliff railway.

Dolores drank late through the night; much merriment ensued,
Until the following morning when a hangover dulled her mood.
During the shenanigans she'd dropped her purse upon the rocks,
"That's it for me," she sadly mused, "they'll put me in the stocks."
Luckily I heard the news and I settled up her bill,
And listening to me teasing helped to bolster up her will.

On night three she chose a site that was quiet, quaint, and sweet,
Right by the rushing streams of stunning Watersmeet.
That evening, I wish I could say that fortune saw her right,
But I'm sorry to report that despite a good old fight,
She lost a tug-of-war against a russet labradoodle,
And ripped apart her make-up bag, the whole kit-and caboodle.

"My mascara, kohl, and eyeshadow! How will I do my eyes?
That talcum powder helped to stop the chafing of my thighs.
You cussèd cur, you furry fiend, you devil of a dog!
If I get my hands on you I will stuff you down the bog!"
But the labradoodle dashed away and disappeared from sight,
His face now rouged and glittered: his owners got a fright.

Undeterred, Dolores tried to chase it through a copse,
Sending hikers scrambling as she slipped up on some moss.
Her finest wig had fallen off, her clothes were torn and ripped,
Her usual polished public face had well and truly slipped.
Finally, she had to admit that dogs love to be chased,
So with grim determination she retraced her steps, shamefaced.

Dolores' luck then worsened when she found to her dismay,
A policeman had turned up and towed her lovely car away.
It was at the pound in Barnstaple – she only had the keys –
To get her little Fiat she would have to beg and plead.
But right now she was stranded here, she looked a frightful scare,
With just the rags she stood in, and no wig to hide her hair.

"I'm a Drag Queen," cried Dolores, "and I never will say never!"
And her subsequent activities were really rather clever.
From her pocket she produced her dire emergency rations,
A packet of pork scratchings and a guide to latest fashions,
A needle and a reel of thread, some sequins, and some glue;
Drag wouldn't be drag if these didn't come along too.

Well what a shock the driver got, aboard bus 309,
When his passenger stepped on in slingbacks tied with twine.
On closer inspection they were made from blocks of wood,
Her wig was made from tufts of grass; it looked reasonably good.
She marched along with confidence, her pace it didn't slacken,
Sequins gaily shimmering on the dress she'd sewn from bracken.

Her tights, it seems, were delicately-woven strands of ivy,
They curled around her legs, and they didn't look too dicey.
And then the pièce de résistance, le magnifique encore,
Was the red clay mud foundation smeared on every pore.

In place of rouge she had smeared liberally on each cheek,
The red juice from ripe berries she'd found growing in the creek.

A burnt stick gave her eyeliner – a spare pair of eyelashes,
Stuck on using sap from trees, eyeshadow made from ashes.
Some clumps of dehydrated moss she'd found upon the ground,
Had proved to be effective as padding, soft and round.
Dolores hadn't finished there, because she's such a goer,
She'd accessorised her outfit with a catkin 'feather' boa.

Somehow Dolores blagged it, she was such a brilliant actor,
She got a lift right into town with a farmer on his tractor.
And then she strode on swiftly, determined she would find,
The policeman who had all her stuff, who'd put her in this bind.
"Barnstaple are you ready?" came her strident battle cry,
"Prepare to surrender this queen's things or otherwise you die!"

A spellbound crowd assessed our girl; it could not be much be plainer,
Dressed like that she had to be a touring entertainer.
They gathered round and waited – would the show be starting now?
Judging her appearance like a champion red poll cow.
"Out of my way!" she bellowed, "you won't believe my tale,
Everything on this here trip has been one great big fail!

"The blasted sea attacked my feet and away my shoes were fleeced,
Then all my bras and knickers were seized by flying beasts.
An evening of debauchery made me think that all was fine,
But it added to my trouble: a hangover from the wine.
The final straw, a mangy mutt that came with thieving jaws,

And took off with all my make-up on its horrid hairy paws."

The crowd were full of sympathy and wowed by her theatrics,
From the youngest little toddler to the oldest geriatrics.
Her histrionics went down well, they loved her hissy fits,
North Devon rarely got to see such glamour and such glitz.
"Bravo!" they squealed, as our girl struck a few more classic poses,
While they screamed for more and showered her with handfuls of red roses.

Our girl had an epiphany and also felt quite flattered,
She realised a designer look wasn't all that mattered.
This crowd loved her for her gall, her shining wit and humour,
And not so much for being a designer-brand consumer.
It wasn't Prada or Versace that made a girl a winner,
She didn't need to go around dressed up like a dog's dinner.

She sashayed out and headed off to Barnstaple town square,
Followed by her loyal crowd as she shook her derriere.
A theatre scout then took his chance and promised her a wage,
That night she wowed the crowds on our own Queen's Theatre stage.
So Dolores lost her heart to our beautiful North Devon,
Our own beloved county, our little patch of heaven.

She said, "It's nothing personal; I really have to stay,"
She hoped that I was well and that I'd visit her some day.
She admitted I'd been right about North Devon, God's own land,
With its countryside, and beaches of stunning golden sand.

Her soft spot, though, was Barnstaple and the good folk of the town,
Who loved her for herself and not the label on her gown.

So now she's still a drag queen, still fabulous is she,
Still glamorous and striking, still fills the crowd with glee.
This is where we'll leave Dolores and her life-affirming story,
Of when she went off camping in all her drag queen glory.
The mishaps she encountered led Dolores to her fate:
Destined to be Devonian – albeit wearing an L-plate!

The Bright Orange Swimming Hat
Irene Sugden

I crept down the uneven concrete slipway towards the beach, painfully aware how hard the incline was on my knees. I braced myself before each step, waiting for the searing pain under each kneecap to take my breath away. I was fully aware that I was waddling like a penguin trying to balance its egg. Menopause combined with onset of old age have a lot to answer for.

As always, Joe was at least ten strides ahead. After nearly forty years of marriage the strides between us were widening in more ways than one.

"Will you just wait, please!" I called but the wind whipped my words away down Westward Ho! beach. Joe eventually stopped and turned to look at me, tapping his right foot impatiently in his oversized, bulbous brown walking boots, hands on hips, looking quite ridiculous with his black woolly hat and steamed-up glasses. He had far longer legs than me and was always in a rush. I ignored his signs of impatience and just kept moving cautiously forward.

The wind was gaining strength and, gusting around the angular slipway, whipped me from all directions. I was so glad I had wrapped up in my North Face coat and black woolly hat. I don't normally wear a hat, but if my hair got wet it would regress to a wild frizz of curls and I had no desire to be mistaken for some mythical sea creature. Oh god! I groaned inwardly as I realised I was dressed in exactly the same outer clothes as Joe. I'd always found it comical when I saw elderly couples out and about in matching attire – now that was us. The realisation had stopped me in my tracks. I shook my head. Not us – surely not! We're not elderly … are we? When did I start to lose my own identity? Anxious to leave that particular thought behind, I started moving forwards again.

As I neared the edge of the slipway I thought I felt rain on my face. Then I realised it was salt spray from waves dashing themselves against the concrete and stone beneath my feet. To the left of the slipway, next to the sea wall, were huge, dark-grey menacing boulders, scarred with the tides of time etched as calling cards from the sea. The boulders were standing shoulder to shoulder like bouncers from a night club trying to prevent the unruly incoming tide. The biggest group of boulders was stacked against the end of the sea wall and had formed a small, sheltered alcove that faced me. The boulders decreased in size across the slipway with the last boulder displaying a red-and-white notice to dog owners.

The tide was coming in fast; surges of white sea spray were rushing over the boulders with great force, and the waves were fighting each other, causing huge crescendos in their efforts to reach the slipway's entrance. Each successive wave gave a watery exhalation as it reached further up the slipway, releasing salty celebrations all over my face then relaxing into stasis before retreating and starting all over again. It was really quite exhilarating.

To the right of the slipway were breathtaking panoramic views along the beach as far as Saunton Sands. The beach itself was virtually submerged by the grey-green sea with its white horses galloping inland, pushing the pebbles up and then dragging them back down noisily from the sea defence ridge that comprised of various shapes and sizes of enormous light grey rocks and pebbles. Many of these were marked with prominent white lines with the additional sprinkle of concrete blocks, driftwood, and other sea debris among them.

Embedded in these rocks and pebbles were long lines of wooden breakers that began to emerge halfway down the ridge and continued down to the beach, evenly spaced, with an array of rounded tips standing to attention like soldiers covered with the green camouflage of seaweed. Each wave was pushing up higher, stretching out its fingertips, trying to grab the top of the ridge then subsiding into temporary submission. I noted, on this side of the slipway, the absence of railings for support or safety – the only concession a bright yellow line painted along its edge.

At last I neared the beach, just as Joe, who had been waiting for several minutes, turned abruptly and stalked back up the incline.

"Thanks for waiting!" I said as he marched past, head down and hands in pockets.

"Too wet and cold down 'ere," he grunted.

"Such a misery!" I growled under my breath.

I decided to stay without him, down by the sea, to absorb the elements. Fleeting smells of salt and seaweed mingled with the sweeping gusts of wind. In the distance was Lundy Island, looking like a black cameo cut-out, ready to be framed, gradually becoming obscured by the increasing low, grey clouds. A seagull flew overhead in silence trying to avoid the irregular thermals, which tossed it around like a kite.

I spotted a solitary small boat a little way out, bobbing frantically up and down as it was pushed from side to side by the waves. The hull was jet black with a white horizontal stripe and bright luminous orange lifeguard rings and buoys tied up at the stern. The small white cabin on top had just enough room for two people. They must be good sailors – or feeling very ill by now, I thought.

The grey skies were full of billowing low clouds thoroughly inspecting the little seaside village. Nothing else stirred but the sea, rumbling and roaring louder on its approach. It was November after all. It was just the two of us – or so I thought.

I decided to turn and follow Joe back up the slipway but stopped at the top to admire the views, taking deep breaths. Bliss! Oh, how my knees felt a sigh of relief from the punishment of the incline. My hands were in my coat pockets, which just about kept them from seizing up with the cold. I wished I'd worn gloves. A flashback of childhood memory conjured the image of my mum telling me, "Keep your hands out of your pockets, just in case you fall over. You will not be able to protect yourself." Protect myself from what? I could still fall and hurt some part of my body, thought old-aged me.

I was startled out of this reverie by a very petite lady, at least as old as me, strutting past in multicoloured leggings – in bright shades of red, purple and orange – a pair of shiny, black, calf-length wellington boots and a giant pink, oversized coat with an even larger hood. I couldn't see her face as she had the hood pulled over her head and her gaze was focused intently on the end of the slipway. A large navy rucksack was over her right shoulder. She continued confidently down to the beach, dropped her rucksack in the alcove of the large boulders, then continued down to where the waves lapped her boots. She looked to her left and right then pulled her hood back, revealing snowy white, short hair. She was wearing black-rimmed sunglasses and light pink lipstick; her face was sun-kissed, as though she had just come back from a holiday abroad.

This stylish vision stared down into the swelling waves, seemingly mesmerised by the sea, as though she was looking for something. I looked away, over towards Saunton Sands in the distance, as I did not wish to impose – although the sight of her in my peripheral vision kept drawing me back. Curious, I decided to resume my observation of this lady, who had by now taken off her glasses together with her coat, revealing a long-sleeved black wetsuit top. She then removed her boots and leggings, exposing two slim, bronzed legs, and pulled on a pair of black wet shoes. Finally, she tucked her hair into a bright orange swimming hat, which had large purple and pink flowers that flapped wildly in the wind. She tucked all her clothing into her rucksack and dropped that, together with her boots, into the alcove between the boulders.

My stomach began to roll with the waves as I realised her intent. Concerned for the sanity of anyone planning to swim in such weather, I edged my way slowly back down the slipway towards her. She must have spotted me – although goodness knows I didn't stick out like she did, in my dowdy coat and hat – because she turned and smiled. She had strikingly blue eyes, complimented with lilac eyeshadow, and tufts of white hair, reminiscent of white feathers, were peeping out from under the swimming hat around her ears.

"You are very brave, going in there!" I said with concern in my voice. "Don't you worry," she answered with a smile, displaying almost perfectly straight teeth. I noticed the light pink lipstick had seeped into the deep lines around her thin lips. "I always check before I go in that it's just right."

"Oh, you swim in the sea often then? The weather is terrible today!" I still displayed my 'concerned' badge in my voice, hoping she might get dressed and get back in the warm. "Yep, every day for the last eighteen years." I couldn't make out her accent; it was soft and strangely reassuring. "Since my husband passed," she continued. "It's good for the mind and soul and not so bad for the body too!" she added with a grin and a glint in her eye. I smiled back, then realised that no one would know she was in the water except myself – and Joe if he had bothered to wait at the top of the slipway for me.

She must have read my mind. "I don't swim on my own. Look over there." She pointed with a bony index finger, complete with scarlet nail polish. I squinted and saw, to my delight, a sleek brown head bobbing in the water a couple of dozen yards out from the beach. A seal! I could just make out its shiny black eyes; long, thick whiskers and the silhouette of its body swaying under the water, in time with the waves.

"Wow! How wonderful!" I gasped.

The lady chuckled. "She is about two years old and waits for me every day when the tide comes in. So I have company: not bad for eighty-two, eh?"

"What a magnificent companion," I replied excitedly and glanced back at Joe to see if he was looking too. There he was, desperately waving his hands at me to come up to the café further up the road that joined the slipway. He had clearly decided he had enough and was becoming hangry, as indicated with the constant jolts of his head to one side for me to join him. He looked comical, as if he were receiving electric shocks.

With an overwhelming sense of sadness I realised he would not be interested in the seal, even if he could see it. My magical moment had been rudely interrupted. I wished I hadn't turned around.

The lady was, by now, making her way down to the water and had put on a pair of black waterproof gloves. I waved as I called out, with a little apprehension, "Lovely to meet you; enjoy your swim!"

She returned the wave with a smile, and continued on her way to meet her swimming buddy.

I walked back up the slipway, deep in thought and touched by the experience, not realising that I was completely wet and starting to feel cold all over. I shivered to think what that brave lady was going to do and stopped abruptly to check she was okay. She was striding into the sea; big waves were lashing up randomly as if trying to grab her little brown legs. Further out, the seal was rolling over and over in the waves, imitating the deathroll of a crocodile, clearly impatient for her playmate.

I looked back up the slope to see that Joe had now disappeared. For a second I wickedly wished he had just popped into oblivion, but in truth I knew the smell of grilled bacon had probably enticed him into the café. To be honest, it was now starting to work its magic on me.

I kept stopping, to make sure I could still see the bright orange swimming hat, as I walked the last few yards to the café, with a final check as I reached the door. There she was, happily swimming quite safely away from the rocks but not too far from the slipway. The seal had swum to meet her and the pair looked quite contented together. An inner feeling of happiness and contentment evaporated all my concerns for this wonderful person, with her contagious joie de vivre. I could make some changes myself, couldn't I? After all, I was nowhere near as old as her – I wasn't done with life yet. I smiled, opened the café door and went in to find Joe.

Soy Un Perdedor
Nathalie Denzey

Hey Jenny B

You're most likely wondering why I'm getting in touch now, more than twenty years after leaving that hellish school on the moors, and I'll admit that it was me being chickenshit that stopped it happening before. I want to say first that what I did, or more didn't do, back then was the most stupid thing I've done and I am so very sorry.

Beck's *Loser* came on the radio this morning and I started singing along without even realising. The words came to me straight away even after all this time. When it got to the line where you and I sang 'saw it off in the dark' I had to stop. Memories came flooding back and I cried for so long. I've googled the lyrics now, and just in case you've ever wondered, it's *'soy un perdedor'* – Spanish for 'I'm a loser', which makes more sense than 'saw it off', and is kind of relevant really.

A picture came into my mind of us sat on your bed, in that seventies mid-terrace in Barnstaple, rewinding the cassette again and again, trying to work out what he was singing. Your dad would be downstairs cooking us the only vegetarian food he knew: bean burgers from the bottom of that knackered old chest freezer. Are you still a veggie? I am. I did start eating meat again a few years back when I was seeing this guy, Alan. Whenever we went to a steak house he would quote this Tibetan monk he'd met when he went travelling in the eighties. 'One death feeds many'. I kind of saw where he was coming from, so we'd do the meal deal whenever we went there, which was quite often. It did taste good. But when Alan disappeared I stopped again. He just vanished, didn't answer any of my calls or texts. That messed me up a fair bit. But I shouldn't complain, especially to you.

I'm single now, have been for a while. Are you still with Matt? It would be awesome if you were. I bet you are. Remember that night the four of us camped on Marine Drive in Woolacombe? Up past the end of the car park and onto that sandy track. Parking side by side with the doors open and music on the stereos. Drinking 20/20 and watching the waves crash so far below as it got dark. Of course you remember. Two tents pitched in the dunes. Me and Stu. You and Matt. Your face the next morning when we walked on the beach and you held me back so you could tell me all about it! I just wish I could go back and tell the 'me' in the other tent what I was supposed to do, not just lie there rigid in a sleeping bag. I literally didn't know that I was supposed to do stuff too! And I'd wondered why Stu wasn't interested after that.

That was the night we stopped being geeks, you and me, wasn't it? We didn't feel out of place, didn't feel so different, because everyone else there was different too. That old club, Marisco, we found just off the main street; the others from school didn't even know about it for a start. It was where you could go and just be yourself, be anyone you wanted. A proper mash up. Just like the music. Do you remember? Primal Scream, Dusty Springfield, The Levellers, Tom Waits, Rage Against The Machine. All of them had something to say, something important to tell us, so we listened, we danced to their songs, shouted their words, on that tiny packed dancefloor, jumped as high as we could, and it was so hot we were all in just vests and shorts, our bare feet sticking to the floor. You'd get *outside and the cold air would dry the sweat on your skin and when your ears stopped ringing you could hear the waves on the beach again.*

That night when the four of us sat around the fire afterwards, and Stu played guitar, was the best night of my life. Even though I didn't know what to do in that tent. I didn't want it to ever end. I still tell people about it now, you know. Even the bit when the ranger told us off the next morning.

I've kept the beautiful photo from the paper of when you got your PhD. I wasn't surprised to see it at all, you stuck at everything, kept on working so hard. You must be something very important now. I know I should have gone to uni, gone to London, too, as we'd planned. I think I felt I needed to keep working on being the person I was becoming, if that makes sense. Still here, still in Woolacombe, still finding my way.

I went back to the club the following summer, every week. I got a job in the Fortescue, just up the road, so I could go straight on after my shift. It was never the same though. Same music, same vibe, but you guys weren't there.

Remember the really tall guy we thought was hot? The one we called Bodhi, he was always right in the middle of the mosh when Killing In The Name was on. He was my first.

I pulled him finally, late that August. I dived in really close to him every time that song played until he noticed me. One night we started kissing on the dance floor then we walked down to the dunes and carried on there, and I was nothing like that time in the tent. We hung out for the rest of the summer. I came along and watched him and his mates surf. We made more fires and smoked weed, drank vodka-and-orange and dropped some tabs. But at the end of the summer he said it wasn't going anywhere. In his words, he had wanted to corrupt me. And he had done. And then he felt bad about it. I guess you never really get to forget where you came from.

Dad got me a job as an au pair in America for a client of his after that. He wanted to get me away from it all, said he hadn't invested all that money in my education so I could doss around with druggies (his words). I lasted six months and came back home.

I've been at this little café ever since, near where I came of age. I've worked my way up to manager. I get six weeks off when it closes in the winter and I go travelling. At least that A in French helps then. The owner's alright. She keeps on at me to go back to my studies though. I said I'll think about it.

I kept all the letters you wrote to me and I am just sorry I didn't write you a single one back. I was so intent on getting rid of all of my old self that I thought I had to get rid of you too.

Your perdedor

Nicci D

Not a Royal Day Out
Ralph Bell-Ley

Her Majesty Queen Elizabeth II was sitting in one of the lounges at Buckingham Palace. She was looking after some of her great-grandchildren: Prince George, Princess Charlotte, and Prince Louis. It was past the children's bedtime – they were all in their pyjamas and dressing gowns – but they were still wide awake and running around, full of energy. Her Majesty knew just what to do.

"Come and sit down," she said to them, "and I shall tell you a story."

The children clambered on to the big red sofa next to the their great-grandmother. The servants had made up the fire in the huge open fireplace, and a tray with cookies and mugs of warm milk had been placed within reach. The Queen handed each child a mug and a cookie and they settled back to listen. This is the story, just as she told it.

* * *

It was in the year 2001, and the middle of summer. The sun was just beginning to rise but I was already up and wide awake. I had spent half the night pacing the long corridors of the palace, thinking over an idea I'd had. I was so excited to share it; I couldn't wait. So I went back into the bedroom and nudged your great-grandfather.

"Philip! Philip! Wake up!" I said, "I have an excellent idea." Philip sat up and had a big stretch, then said, "I`m all ears, my darling."

I sat down on the end of the bed with a big smile on my face. I said, "Well Philip, sometimes I wonder what it would be like to be out there, you know, with the public, without anyone knowing us."

Philip's brow furrowed as he shook his head in confusion. "But how would we do that, my dear?" he asked.

"I have it all planned out," I said. "It will take a couple of days to get everything arranged but I have already invited a specialist make-up artist, from a movie company, to come along and see us."

"This sounds jolly fun!" said Philip. "We could have a lovely day out together with no one knowing who we are."

It was just after lunch that day when our butler, Perkins, announced a visitor.

"Your Majesty: a Mr Luxton. He claims you have requested his attendance."

"Oh good," I said. "Yes I did; send him in please,"

Mr Luxton was the make-up artist. As he entered the room, I dismissed Perkins with instructions that we should not be disturbed. I swore our guest to secrecy and explained my plan to him.

"Prince Philip and I would like to have a day out together, but we do not want anyone to notice us. We do not want anyone to join us – none of our helpers, no butlers, no security, and no press, just us! Can you help disguise us please? You will be well rewarded. But under no circumstances should anyone know what we are doing, is that understood? And I would like to call this Operation D.O.T."

With a big grin on his face Mr Luxton said, "Sure, I can do this for you. I am the best in the industry; I can totally change your appearance so that no one will know who you are." He took measurements and photographs of our faces, so that he could go away and work on our disguises. He said he would be back six o'clock the next morning to get us ready for our adventure.

Once Mr Luxton had left, your great-grandfather turned to me and asked, "Where would you like to go, Elizabeth?"

I didn't hesitate. "Devon," I said. "I would like to go back to Devon. Of all the places we have visited on our official trips, all around the world, Devon is my favourite place of all."

Philip agreed at once. He was really getting into the spirit of it now. "With our disguises we could use public transport and go on the Great Western Railway," he said, rubbing his thighs in excitement. "But what was that about Operation D.O.T.? What does that mean?"

"D.O.T. stands for Day Out Together," I explained. "Now pay attention; we will need aliases so that when we are out amongst the public, people will not get suspicious. I have already chosen a name for you; you're going to be Frank. You look like a Frank, and sometimes you act like that Frank on the television back in the '70s."

With a grin, your great-grandfather said, "Very well, then I'm going to call you Betty." I opened my mouth to protest, but Philip held up a hand. "We've been married too long for me to start calling you by another name now," he said. "It's bound to slip out at some point; you know what I'm like. No, if this Mr Luxton does his job properly nobody will guess Betty is the Queen of England."

The next day I gave instructions to Perkins that we were not to be disturbed at all, telling him that we both needed a 'duvet day'. I'd heard the term on a television show and thought it sounded fun. I'm sure I saw his eyebrows raise just slightly when I said it, but he bowed and agreed to pass the message to the rest of the staff.

Mr Luxton arrived right on time to put our disguises in place. It was quite marvellous! He made me look at least ten years younger and gave me very dark skin, as though I had been on a long holiday in the sun somewhere. And he put a purple rinse on me; I really did look completely different. He made your great-grandfather look much younger too. It was very impressive. "I can't remember when I last had hair like this," he said, laughing.

Mr Luxton explained that changing our face and hair was only part of the disguise; if we were really going to carry this off we'd have to change our voices and wear different clothes. He gave us both an outfit for the day, with cash in the pockets – spending money, he called it – and we had a little practise with our new South London accents. He was happy that we'd got it about right when I told him, "You're gonna luv it when you see the next Honours List!"

We sneaked out of our suite and out to the nearest exit without being noticed. We even passed Perkins on one of the stairways – he must have thought we were early-morning cleaners. We were giggling quietly the whole way. We took a taxi to Paddington Station and I must say the London cabbie was very entertaining. He told us lots of stories about me that I'd never heard before!

I was surprised to see no flowers or carpets laid out at the station, but Philip said he thought they are only put there when there's an 'R' in the month – who knew? The smell of the diesel trains and the heat was quite intense, and it was terribly busy. We queued for the ticket office and bought two returns to Exeter St David's.

On the train, we shared a table with a nice, chatty young couple, who asked where we were heading.

"We're off to Devon for a day out aren't we, Frank?" I said.

"Yes, Betty," said your great-grandfather, with a very convincing glottal stop, "but I dunno what we're doing when we get there."

The young couple suggested we go to North Devon and we both recalled that we had been there once before, when we visited Barnstaple in 1956.

"Why not try Westward Ho! this time, then," said the young man. "It'll take a couple of hours from Exeter – nothing happens very fast in Devon – but you can try a Hockings ice cream while you're there." That decided us. At the palace we have to eat our ice creams out of cut-glass bowls with tiny silver spoons, and we longed for a cornet.

Before long we were in Barnstaple and nobody had recognised us – Operation D.O.T. was working! We hopped on a number 21 bus, where we encountered our first difficulty: the driver wanted to see our bus passes. I told him that Frank had forgotten them. Philip – Frank – got a bit carried away with his character acting. "Oh, Betty," he said, "I'm sorry, but I've had a lot of harassment lately." The driver tutted and nodded his head towards two empty seats across the gangway. We'd got away with it – it was really quite exhilarating!

Westward Ho! was heavenly and the weather was perfect: blue sky with not a cloud in sight. We wandered along the seafront, hand-in-hand, full of smiles at the thought of a day's freedom. We wanted to pack as much into it as we possibly could. First stop was the crazy golf course.

Philip took charge of the score card – I like to let him have the upper hand in some things – and we strode out to tackle the first hole. As we had never played the game before, it did take us a bit of getting used to, but we were both laughing and having fun the whole way around. By the time we reached the last hole we both had the same score. I was up first and I managed a hole in one! Philip was gracious in his praise, but I knew he would beat me if he could so, just as he started to swing his club for the final shot, I pinched his bottom! His ball flew high into the air, in completely the wrong direction. We both cried with laughter.

Next stop was the amusement arcade. "Let's see what this is all about," said Philip. As we walked in we were dazzled by the lights flashing from all the slot machines and games. There was music playing, and there were so many people having fun. Your great-grandfather wanted to have a go on the 2p slots, so he put his hand in his pocket and picked out a pound coin. He nudged me and whispered, "There's a picture of you on the back of this coin."

"Behave yourself, Frank," I said in my best South London voice, to put off anyone who had overheard.

He put the coin in the change machine but didn't put a cup under it, so a load of 2p coins poured out and went all over the place. That set us off in fits of giggles again. We spent a whole hour in the arcade, playing different games and having a wonderful time. As we left, we spotted the Hockings ice cream van that the young man had mentioned earlier. We joined the queue and waited our turn – another new experience.

As the gentleman handed me my cone (a 99 with clotted cream – delicious!) he gave me a cheeky wink. "Nice hair, Ma'am," he said. "A bit of colour looks good on you." Then he smiled and turned to the next customer. I could have kissed him!

We found a bench overlooking the sea and sat there to enjoy our ice creams, happy as can be, before taking the long journey back home. We both agreed we had had the best day ever, and that we would do it again, at least once, every summer.

* * *

As the Queen looked down, she realised that all three children had fallen fast asleep on the sofa next to her. She tucked a blanket over them and tiptoed out to find Perkins, who was waiting patiently just outside the door.

"Ask Nanny to carry the children to their beds, please," she told him, before adding, "Oh – and please see that Philip and I are not disturbed tomorrow: we'll be having another duvet day."

The Phoenix
Darren Colwill

Many people believe that scientists are the cleverest people on our planet, and yet they are arguably always wrong. Scientists in ancient Greece believed that the world was the centre of the universe and that everything else moved around it. For a long time people also believed it was flat. They were eventually proved wrong by people such as Kepler. Kepler's work influenced Sir Isaac Newton, and his 'laws' of gravity and other work, which backed up the idea that the world was in fact not the centre of the universe at all and was more like a large blue football. This is pretty much what we believe today and it's actually correct, because that is what the schools teach us as fact. A fact is a thing that is known or proved to be one hundred percent true, and you cannot argue with it.

Or can you?

Who is to say that the Earth is round and that we don't live in the centre of the Universe? Well, astronauts maybe. They have been outside of our atmosphere and have seen the blue sphere with their own eyes. Fair enough. But how do they know that we are not in the centre of the universe? We have not found all of its edges yet and got our large tape measure out to measure, have we? And then of course there are the unknown factors, like black holes. And we can't assume that our limited human eyes see the world for what it really is.

Scientists know nothing. They claim that the smallest thing in the world is an electron. That's what they claim, and some even claim it as fact. They, however, are wrong. As is anybody else who claims anything is fact. It is fact that nothing is fact. And that fact is only really, at best, a guess.

This, then, means that the story I am about to tell you could very easily be true; indeed, scientists cannot prove it wrong.

* * *

In a south-westerly sloping field, a mile outside of Iddesleigh, Cow 162 was grazing. It was mid-morning and 162 was having an average day. Unbeknown to her, orbiting her left ear was a planet smaller than an electron. Cow 162 was entirely unaware of it, but there it was. These planets are actually rather common and are all around us, orbiting random parts of our bodies. Maybe one day scientists will be able to build a telescope powerful enough to detect them. But for the moment they can't. You will just have to take my word for it that it was there.

The particular planet that orbited Cow 162 was home to many different walks of life, but its oldest inhabitant was the phoenix.

* * *

The world is actually rather small when you look at it. Well at the very least it is when you look at it from a distance. That's what the phoenix thought, as he flew high up into the clouds above the solid earth. That's the way he saw it most of the time.

"I'm only small compared to many other creatures and yet I can see the tops of huge mountains, sections of oceans and even a multitude of countries at one time. It must be horribly cramped to be one of those big creatures," he muttered to himself.

It was true. There were many larger creatures then the somewhat diminutive phoenix, and yet many if not all of them disagreed with him. The phoenix could not comprehend that the other creatures on the world could spend their whole lives travelling and still not see all of it. But of course, no other creature had been on the planet as long as him and had not had the time to be able to see the amount of things he had. Then again, most of the mountains and oceans hadn't either. This then demonstrated that space and time was completely the opposite way around to the phoenix. For him, time would go on forever but space was a restriction. Though this was not the right time to think of such things, he reflected.

The phoenix was increasingly anxious and tired. His rebirth was going to be soon – far too soon for his liking. He needed to find a place where he could perch himself. His rebirth had caught him unawares, but at his current body's age and mental state, most things caught him unawares. This was most likely due to the fact that this particular incarnation had been a bit more stressful than any he had experienced before. It had made him forgetful, clumsy and, worst of all, tired.

Instinct had led him closer to the solid earth, where he had found himself circling above an opening in a small, peaceful beech wood. He thought that it would be pleasant to rest his grey-tipped wings for a bit. As he glided lower, targeting an opening in the tree canopy, he spotted something glinting in the sunlight. Was he lucky enough to have found a lovely pool to bath in before his rebirth?

He circled lower and lower, until the trees began to rise around him. He alighted on a branch, high enough to keep an eye out for any ravenous animal that might be passing. This precaution was not taken out of fear of being eaten and killed. No, he was a phoenix; no physical animal could kill him. It was just he had been caught by surprise a few times before and had on many occasions been swallowed whole. It really was quite an unpleasant experience for all concerned.

That had happened a lot in this current incarnation, now that he came to think about it. Maybe that was why it had felt such a stressful cycle. He had not yet discovered an animal whose insides could be described as first-class accommodation. Besides, he was of no nutritional gain to anything that did try and eat him; there had not been an animal to date that had successfully digested him. This only left a horrible process in which the poor ignorant creature had to regurgitate him. Although, he thought, there was that one occasion, where a poor dragon had swallowed him whole for breakfast. No matter how hard the dragon tried to eject him, the phoenix could not get back up its neck. Stomach surgery had been the only option, which sadly resulted in the ill-fated dragon having an even larger hole to fill. The phoenix still felt horribly guilty and embarrassed about the whole situation.

He looked down from his perch and smiled smugly to himself. He had been right: there was a charming pool he could bath in. The water sparkled a mirrored reflection back up to his deteriorating eyes. He groaned aloud as he took in the image. His feathers had lost their energetic golds and their burning reds. Now there were hints of grey amongst what could be described as lethargic yellow and burnt-out brown. He was truly feeling like an old soul.

A jolt of pain pulsated up his spine as the image in the water blurred, his eyes straining to focus, before failing altogether. His death before life was suddenly upon him.

"Damn it!" he swore, as his breath grew ragged, "Sooner than I thought …"

He tried to brace himself, but it was no good. His body had already gone into shock. His heart began to pound out of his feathered breast. It was trying to get as many beats in as it could before its demise. Time slowed for the phoenix and the world around him dawdled with it. The slight breeze around his feathers evaporated. The noises of the woodland birds receded. His awareness shrank until it took in only the space he needed in the Universe. His bodily functions were failing.

The phoenix had experienced death many times, but it never got any easier. He knew he would live again, and yet he still felt scared as his body began to heat up. He raised his wing tips in front of him. Flames sprang to life on top of them, with energetic sparks like two flints smashing together. The fire began to spread. Down his wings it went: a plague of fire engulfing his body. The pain was excruciating. He squawked out loud. To the outside world it would have been a wonderful sight to see, the rebirth of a phoenix: a scene full of energy, excitement and colour. To him it was hell.

The fire was soon above, below, around and within his entire body. It was heat beyond description. The flames burnt hotter, from red to orange. The pain was still there. Hotter: from orange to yellow. The pain was still there. Yellow to white. The sheath of pain was still there and the flames grew higher. The heat sizzled his feathers away, leaving the phoenix naked. His skin was now blackening, burning, smouldering. He could smell his flesh cooking. He wanted to vomit, but he was too weak, too tired, to scared. Why could it not be over already?

His body finally consumed, only smoke and the last flickering flames could be seen by the puzzled birds looking on from the nearby trees.

Blackness.

His death was imminent. Panic took hold of him. But was death not what he craved more than anything now? At last there was relief, the pain had somehow subsided. He began to feel very numb.

Death.

* * *

Life.

Solid white brightness covered his eyes like a blanket. Forever it felt; seconds it lasted. Colour came back. A reflection! That is what he remembered. His eyesight came into focus. He was looking upon the surface of the pool once more, as sunlight twinkled on the rippling surface. He breathed out. He breathed in. He began to feel his new body.

He puffed out his chest and stretched his talons out. It felt effortless to move his limbs; they were young again. No more pain from his joints! He spread out his wings majestically, revealing a beautiful arrangement of gold and red feathers. He then looked down at his outstretched talons. They were as sharp as a sword, and as deadly.

He then became aware of the sounds around him. His hearing was in tune with the music of the world, more than ever he could remember. He focused his ears to the sound of some startled birds in the trees. They were looking at him, confused at the commotion that their distant cousin, the firebird, had just created.

"Funny," the phoenix said to himself. "I had not noticed them there before." Astonishment took him as he heard his own voice. It was not croaky, slow and doddery anymore. The sound waves from his syrinx now vibrated and projected out like the voice of an operatic tenor. He was young again. A new life had started for him. He flapped his wings and flew up into the tree canopy. His strokes were clumsy and he staggered in the breeze to begin with, but he continued to rise up higher and higher until he was above and beyond the trees again, elevated above the landscape. He would soon get used to his new wings, he knew. They just needed a bit of time. They were young, and eager, wanting to fly, flutter, float, hover, glide, drift, sail and soar. Excitement blasted out of his new heart as he began to think about the wonder of his new life cycle. He was going to have new adventures, he was sure, in this small and perfect world that he knew so well.

* * *

Cow 162 looked up. She had just experienced a funny itch by her left ear. As she refocused on the field around her she noticed a crow sat on an old wooden gate looking away from her. The crow did nothing of any particular interest. She huffed and flicked her ear as if to remove the strange sensation and went back to grazing.

A Roman in Devon
Darren Colwill

If Lucius had not been running for his life, he might have found the frosty autumn sunrise a stunning sight. The Dumnonii druids were tracking him, looking to send him to the world after life. Lucius, however, was not ready to die yet. Not like this. Not so far from home. Not so far from his wife and son. How he wished to hold them both in his arms right now!

The only one of his squadron left alive, he had dumped his armour a while back so as to cover ground faster in just his sun-bleached red tunic. With only his sword for defence, and a small pouch of dried meat to sustain him, he would need to use all his experience and strength to find his way back to Isca, the most westerly Roman stronghold in the province of Britannia.

Lucius had been a *speculator*, a scout, for the mighty Roman Empire since 35 AD and he had proven himself for sixteen years. He was among the best *speculatores* the army had, and he had the *phalerae* to prove it – medals won as he established his reputation from the Germania campaign all the way to this savage Britannia. But the south-westerly province of Dumnonia was his hardest mission so far. How had he lost all of his legionaries? Was this going to be his last mission for his beloved empire? And how was he going to get back to camp?

He did not know the answer to these questions yet. All he knew was he was not ready to die.

The land of Dumnonia had been full of surprises. His centurion had misjudged the challenges a late-season scouting mission in this wild and mysterious land would bring. The terrain was unpredictable, changing dramatically from one league to the next: ancient oak forests, bleak moors, rolling hills and deep valleys – all sandwiched between two seas.

Lucius had lost his horse and his unit a day ago: his horse, shot with arrows as he tried to escape the mysterious druids his scouting unit had stumbled into. The same druids had slaughtered his men and now wished for his death. They knew the landscape better than he did and were not stupid enough to wade straight into a bog. He had been ploughing through it for the last mile, he judged, and lost his boots within the first fifty paces. No longer was he a mighty Roman solder; he was just a man fighting to get home. His legs felt heavier than some of the granite rocks on the nearby moorland. His eyelids felt similarly weighty.

He stopped and scanned the forbidding landscape surrounding him. Curse the gods! He was lost: a hard truth for a scout to admit. His head drooped to his chest; his Roman arrogance had been his downfall. His unit had left camp on horseback, a full cavalry squadron of the Roman Empire in full armour. They believed the visual impact would be enough to intimidate the local barbarians. They were wrong.

He sucked the musty cold air into his lungs to calm his nerves. "Stop dwelling on what has been done, Lucius," he muttered to himself. "You will survive. You are a good Roman. The gods look favourably on you." He pulled a leg free from the mire, glanced up at the rising sun, adjusted his course and struck out once more.

The sun was nudging the treetops when Lucius cleared the bog. He settled into a faster gait, although the going on this harder ground was stony, slicing his bare feet into bloody strips. Ignoring the pain, he pushed on to the crest of a hill. He stopped. Looked down. Smiled. The valley bottom glinted silver.

Reaching the river, Lucius threw himself to the edge of the bank to drink and cool his head and his arms. Shaking like a dog, he plunged in to continue upstream. With no sign of his pursuers, this was his last safety measure; he felt sure, now, that he would make it back to the stronghold. The river water soothed his bloodied feet but it was slow going and ice-cold so, when he felt he had gone far enough to throw off any tracker, he clambered out to pick up the pace on dry land.

The sun was high now, and bright in his eyes. The oak woodland up ahead would make good cover for a break. Lucius reached the first stand of trees and lowered himself to sit with his back against a sturdy trunk, relieved to take pressure off his feet. The dried meat he pulled from his pouch was not appetising, but he could almost hear his stomach shout for joy as the food reached it. He then began to cut away at his tunic, producing two long pieces of cloth which he wrapped around his feet.

The ground cover in the wood was sparse. Drifting leaves littered the forest floor, broken up by occasional holly bushes, bracken, and immature hazel trees. Despite the bindings, his feet were in a poor shape, and he needed to do whatever he could do to protect them. He shivered, suddenly aware of how bitterly cold the air it was, now that he had stopped running. A howl from a distant wolf startled him. In broad daylight? His scalp prickled. What devilry was this? Time to move on.

Morning stretched into noon, and he had made good progress. Despite this, Lucius' instincts told him he was still being followed. Had those devilish druids sent a demon or spirit after him? A shiver ran slowly down his spine as he heard an unnatural sound behind him. It was not his imagination: something *was* following him again. He picked up the pace, jogging and ducking between the trees. He heard rustling. Something large crashing through the undergrowth. Closer.

Whack!

Everything went dark. All senses lost.

* * *

Cold on his back. He was lying on the ground. Lucius opened his eyes to see a heavy branch above him. He must have run into it. Idiot! He growled in pain as he sat up, then realised the sound was being matched by something to his left.

A huge black wolf stalked into his field of vision, piercing yellow eyes full of hatred, bristling hairs raised high along its hunched back. A creature from hell. The beast began to move forward, step by careful step. Lucius sent a silent prayer to the gods, a request that he might survive to see his wife and son once more, as he felt for his sword – but found nothing. The wolf lifted its lip in a savage snarl, showing murderous white fangs. Lucius strained to stand up but his body had given in and he could only shuffle backwards until his back pushed against the bole of an ancient oak. He could go no further. He was exhausted – and trapped. Knowing that death was surely upon him, Lucius began to pray aloud, as tears blurred his vision. He was a failure to his son and his wife and to the Roman Empire.

He wiped at his face. The blurred shape of the wolf was padding closer. But now, seemingly out of nowhere, another figure – tall, dark and hooded – was standing behind it. A Dumnonii druid.

"*Mac Tíre*," the druid whispered softly. The wolf stopped in its tracks. The druid raised their long, thin arms high above their head, then dropped them with lighting pace towards Lucius. The world around him suddenly went dark.

* * *

Lucius woke, disorientated and confused. His stomach convulsed. He turned to his left side and vomited. Watery bile splattered to the side of him. The steam from it rose up into his nostrils as the acidic taste and smell burnt the back of his throat and nose.

As he tried to move away from his excreted stomach acid he realised that he was tied to the ground. He lifted his head as far as he could. It throbbed as he tried to take in his surroundings. It was a clear night above him and bright stars shone down, illuminating a number of mature trees circling him. He lay in the middle of a clearing within a circle of torches on stakes, their flames burning steadily in the still night. Dispersed between the stakes stood a dozen dark-cloaked Dumnonii, staring in at him.

Lucius' heart leapt like a frightened deer.

He tilted his head to the right and immediately recognised the figure of the tall, thin Dumnonii that had struck him out cold, now standing beside a large, flat-topped stone, less than two paces away. The figure still had their hood up but from Lucius' angle he could make out long facial features in the torch light. Eyes penetrated deep as they bore into Lucius. This was clearly a man of power and influence.

A deep drum began to pound like an earthquake in his ears.
Boom! ... *Boom!* ... *Boom!*

The cloaked locals, inspired by the rhythmic drone, began a deep, whispered chant. The same words, over and over ... Lucius was able to pick out some of the words. Four in particular cut through him like sharp Roman steel.

"*Immsoí ... kerrek ... deamhan ... scrios ...*" The Dumnonii sang. "Turn ... stone ... demon ... kill ..."

What horror were they planning? Despair erupted from Lucius as he contemplated his fate. "Please, spare me!" he cried out. "Please! I will give you gold. Just let me go. I—"

"Stop, beast!" The man to his right cut him off in Lucius' own Latin. "Do not try to tempt me, demon. I know your motives and we will not appease you."

"Y-you can understand me? Who are you? Where am I?" Lucius stammered with shock.

"Yes, demon, I can understand you. We are not as barbaric as you may believe. We are a strong, intelligent, courageous people. We are the inhabitants and caretakers of this beautiful land and you, you are a demon. You come here and you disregard our ways. You seek to force yourself upon the land that is ours.

"I am Kenver – great chief in your language – and you are in the land we call *Sceft beara* – Shebbear in your tongue. It is a spiritual place where the gods have blessed us with the mightiest wood to craft our staves: strong and dependable, much like my kin around me. And tonight it will be the place where we trap your demon ways and prevent you from doing further harm."

With that, Kenver stood up over Lucius' head. "*Thig suas,*" he said in a powerful voice. The others strode forth, each with a long oakwood staff, and crowded around the massive stone slab beside him, slamming them underneath in unison.

"Time to die, demon," Kenver whispered, looking deep into Lucius' eyes.

They were going to turn the stone onto him. Lucius tried to still the tremors that wracked his body. He was scared, yes, but he was a Roman and a proud one. He did not want these Dumnonii to see his fear. His imminent death would not be dignified, but it was in the line of duty as a Roman soldier and he was not a coward.

"*Hēv!*" Kenver shouted. And so they heaved.

"*Hēv!*" Kenver shouted again. The slab started to lift on the side farthest from Lucius. He closed his eyes and thought of his beautiful wife and his strong son.

"*Hēv!*" The voice of the druid was all he could hear now, as the stone tilted higher with the combined efforts of the Dumnonii.

"*Hēv!* ... *Hēv!*"

The stone reached its tipping point and Lucius took in one last gasp of air, closing his eyes. The stone crashed down onto him. He heard his own ribs crack and felt pain like no other as every inch of air was forced out of his lungs. His desperate attempts to inhale were futile. His struggles did not last long.

Kenver looked down at the dead Roman, satisfied with the night's work. He spoke to his people.

"Tonight we have trapped the demon and we have stopped our land from being plagued by his darkness. But the demon spirit is cunning: I decree that the devil stone must be turned each year, at this time, to keep this wickedness at bay. Promise me, my people, that you will do this. Promise me that you will tell your children – and their children's children – to turn the stone."

Under the Spreading Oak
Jane Bheemah

The last vestiges of night cloak the woods in shadow. No sound, save for the tramp of boots as the gamekeeper makes his pre-dawn round, checking on the pheasants in their pens. Its hunt disturbed, a fox slinks by, picking up a new scent as the rabbit it almost had vanishes into a burrow. There is movement in the undergrowth; a fieldmouse flees from Monsieur Renard's razor-sharp teeth. Saved – for now. The predator must look elsewhere. Keeping my vigil, I feel my boughs shiver in the breeze. I've heard it said that little has changed here since the first map of Powderham was drafted in 1723.

I hear the whoosh of an early train as it shoots down the Paddington to Penzance line that runs close to the river. Once through the sleepy village of Starcross, it will hug the coast all the way to Cornwall. Inky blackness gives way to an opalescent, grey light as a pale moon rides high above the castle. A ribbon of silver, the Exe flows out to sea, a few small fishing boats dotted on the horizon. Around my sturdy trunk the rough grass lies, damp with dew. Then, like a soft breath, comes sunrise, painting the sky in delicate hues of pink and gold. The sighing wind rustles through my leaves as the hours pass.

A May morning like any other. My branches reach up to the cerulean sky. There's a shimmer of mist over the Exe now. Here in the Powderham deer park, set in deepest Devon, the seasons come and go like an eternal wheel. I'm one of the forest giants, standing sentinel and watching the days unfurl. I've lost count of the springs I've seen as the cold earth warms, and a carpet of bluebells spreads out on the woodland floor. All life is played out here. Young lovers wander the well-worn track, with eyes only for each other, whispering promises and secrets they know I will never tell. I've come to recognise love that will last a lifetime – and love that is destined to wither like tender buds at the first sign of frost.

The place is alive with birdsong. A couple of ramblers stop, marvelling at my width and the texture of my bark. They wonder aloud how old I am. I listen to the answer for, though I must be ancient, I confess I do not know how old I am. Sometimes it feels like eons.

All I know is that my roots go deep. I've been here ever since, as a tiny acorn asleep in the earth's dark womb, I awoke and pushed my way to the surface. How did I know to do that? A mystery even to me but do it I did. Finding there was light and space to grow, I stretched – a memory that is as clear as if it happened yesterday. Then slowly, ever so slowly over the decades, I became taller, wider, and bushier. In winter I lose my leafy costume but in spring my foliage returns and I am swathed in green again.

"It's easy, mate. You tell the age of a tree by the circles on its trunk." One of the ramblers pats me with a rough hand. "This one's an oak. They've existed long before humans. And this fine specimen's been on the planet longer than you or me, Fred. Though I guess you'd have to cut it down and count those rings inside to really know."

I tremble at the mention of being hewn down. A woodcutter sent to topple me only to discover how old I am! These things happen; it's not my wild imagining. I dread such chance remarks as, "Oh, is that tree listing?" Folk need caution. Words can prove fatal. Last winter there was a storm that lit up the heavens, thunder rolling in from the Haldon Hills. Jagged streaks of lightning ripped up the sky. My companion, an elegant horse chestnut, was felled after being struck, the tips of its tall branches all twisted and blackened. Stunted, it could have survived, yet 'unsafe' was the verdict. "May fall …" I heard the park ranger say and, "Dangerous: too close to the path." I still hear the echo of a groan as my old friend crashed to the ground and try hard not to look at the gap that's been left.

"Oaks can live five hundred years, or more."

The other hiker frowns. "Aren't some of the oldest oaks in the country found here on the Powderham Castle estate?"

Agreeing, the first man announces that oak is one of the most durable timbers and was used to build HMS Victory, Lord Nelson's flagship. This sounds impressive!

My interest piqued, I listen on. Apparently, wine is aged in oak barrels, and the toughness of my wood makes it ideal for burial caskets … though I prefer not to think of that last detail. Consulting their guidebook, the hikers look towards the castle and move on, stepping aside as the *clip-clop* of hooves heralds the approach of horses. The riders are the Earl of Devon and the Countess, returning to Powderham stables after exercising two of their finest mounts. The gelding, black as midnight and nostrils flaring, trots past. The bay mare tosses her fine head and whinnies. I fancy it's a call to me.

A small group of teenagers appear, bringing laughter and energy as they flop down on the grass. My green boughs afford them shade. Coming from the surrounding area, they are in their final year of study at Teignmouth Community College. Most are familiar to me; they have often hung out in the deer park over the last few turns of the year's wheel. However, I sense a more serious air now. Exams are ahead, and decisions must be made about what to do when the textbooks are put away. The wind of change will blow whether they are ready for it or not.

Amid the casual banter I hear new words being spoken, like job, gap year and uni application. It's easy to tell the ones who, like nervous fledglings, are destined to fly. Yet what will happen to the others, the ones who don't quite make it? Tom, the gamekeeper's boy, concerns me the most. He's a smart lad if he puts his mind to it, but his mind is elsewhere. Mostly on a leggy blonde called Laura, with baby-blue eyes and a tumbling mass of sun-kissed hair.

Laura's flame burns bright. She's a natural-born flirt, a girl who has no notion of the hurt she may cause. She and Tom have become a pair, but I know she won't stay long with him. It's not in her nature. This girl is feisty like a headstrong filly. No matter, for there's fever in the air. Spring burgeons, and Tom is bewitched.

Hovering on the edge of the group is Ruby, her sweet face flushed like the bloom of a rose. A perfect foil for Laura's fairness, Ruby's dark locks shine like a conker. Quiet and gentle, I wonder if it is only me who can see the yearning in her face. Her limpid, brown eyes follow Tom's every move. This is a lass who would offer him her heart, if only he let her. But, though he may give her a nod, or throw her a grin, she hardly exists for him.

They meet here regularly, these young folk, to sprawl under my spreading branches and talk. As if by osmosis, their vitality seeps into my gnarled, old bones. As my sap rises I feel their energy renew me. Oh, I give what shelter I can when the storm clouds gather and a hard rain starts to fall. Yet I know life will take them and shake them. What I can do? Nothing, save stand sentinel and watch as I've always done, as yellow primroses nestle in the undergrowth, and overgrown hedges burst with hawthorn and cow parsley.

Late spring slips into summer and the swallows return from their wintering in South Africa. Exams done, there is only the waiting for results now. Laura isn't worried. Instead she's restless, keen for adventure. I sense her energy pulling away. She will be the first to take flight; unlike Ruby, a shy homebird, life in a West Country village has become stale for her. As the group pass round a few illicit cans of drink, Laura talks about drama school and London, where she plans to go in September. Tom is anxious, I sense it, belatedly wishing he'd studied more. However, time moves forward, not back. First love is magical, but seldom lasts. He must know there will be a parting of ways.

The bright sunshine glints on Powderham Castle, throwing it into sharp relief. No rain for a while, the earth is packed hard in the arid ground. I am proud to stand here, one of the estate's finest broadleaf oaks. I glimpse the Belvedere Tower, a landmark in its own right. Not far away from me purple foxgloves grace the bank of a meandering stream. I see families strolling through the deer park, children racing ahead, eager to see the majestic stags and hinds in the distance. Pale gingery brown, with white spots on their backs and black-and-white tails, I've heard the gamekeeper say that these are fallow deer. Fenced off from the public right of way, the animals roam undisturbed.

The summer is long and sweet. It's for tanned, sturdy-limbed youths and girls in swirly cotton dresses. Tom and Laura steal away on their own sometimes. I watch them wander along a different path, fingers entwined as they whisper to each other. Every so often Tom leans in close to kiss her. Her giggles reach me on the balmy breeze. He is in thrall to her. She, in turn, is not unaware of the power she wields.

Until one day I don't see them anymore. The young ones don't come. August melts into September, hardly missing a beat. The hedgerows are bursting with berries as the season ends. Like fire in the heavens, the sunsets are vivid and red. Slowly, the evenings draw in. Autumn slips over the threshold, bringing the scent of woodsmoke in its wake. There's a mellowness now, and a glorious tapestry of colour. My foliage changes from green to shades of crimson, orange and brown – before, dry as parchment, my leaves wither and fall.

October is the month of the deer rut, the breeding season. Their broad, palmate antlers grown, the stags are at their most magnificent now. Fawns will be born the next summer. Weather and ground conditions permitting, the castle runs the last of the ever-popular deer safaris.

Then one day Tom reappears, the same and yet changed. His aura is different. He walks alone, kicking at a pile of dry leaves as he takes a short cut home. His shoulders droop. There is sadness in his eyes and I know without telling that Laura has gone.

Daylight is fading. A murmuration of starlings swoop and dive in the evening dusk. The woods are still at night, hushed, like a thief keeping a watchful wait. I see a sliver of moon and then, one by one, a sprinkling of stars. The shadow of a barn owl glides by on silent wings, focused on its hunt.

November brings fog and sleet and short, dark days. There's a chill in the air. Overnight the temperature drops to zero. I see a glitter of frost in the mornings and the sheen of ice on puddles. An easterly wind blows off the estuary, sweeping down the valley and making ramblers huddle in their coats. The sensible ones remember to wear hats and scarves. Some folk collect fir cones to bring home and dry by the hearth, ready to paint silver and gold for Christmas decorations. They'll return in December for armfuls of mistletoe and holly.

Cawing rooks, glossy and black, gather on my bare branches. I offer what shelter I can, but oaks are deciduous, and this is the harsh, die-back time. All my leaves have fallen, and with no protection the cold gnaws at my ancient bones. I stand resolute and strong as the winter winds howl and gales blow up the estuary from the sea.

January brings a flurry of snow, powdery and white. Snowdrops and crocuses circle my trunk now. In the field close by I hear the bleating of sheep, no doubt glad of their thick, woolly fleeces. The farmer makes his rounds and checks, but luckily, no lambs have been born in this cold snap. They would struggle to survive. Suddenly, there is the sound of running feet and I recognise laughter on the crisp air.

Tom appears, jogging down the track with Ruby. Enjoying the snow, they pause, easy in each other's company. He's teasing her about something, hence the laughter. They both have a lightness of being I haven't seen for a while. Stopping under my branches, I hear Tom clear his throat and suggest a date next weekend – a film they're both keen to see is being shown at the Exeter Picture House. Pulling her bobble hat on tighter, Ruby nods. Tom grins. Bolder now, he mentions grabbing a pizza at The Waterfront down on the quay afterwards. If she'd fancy that? Her answering smile is like sunshine after rain.

I watch him, hesitant at first, stoop to kiss her. She reaches up, not hesitant at all, and kisses him in return. Then, fingers entwined, they move on.

The days lengthen and, perennial as the grass, come the first signs of spring. February slips into March and all at once it's April again. Another year has gone full circle. I'm here as I've always been, standing sentinel, keeping my vigil in the Powderham deer park.

A Serene Affair
Ella-Jane Hobson

The sun gently kissed the horizon as it began its embrace with the depths. It was a serene affair, made up of soft blues that gradually darkened as the light faded. Rippling waves caressed the shore as the tide crept forward.

There was no rush. Even the wind was taking a leisurely pace as it brushed against the cliff face, ambling across the cove and onwards to wherever it wished. Each moment stretched out forever, broken up by the occasional bird cry before returning into its endlessness. Time didn't exist here. It didn't need to.

A seal head popped out of the water, breaking the surface as it came up for air. It dipped back under briefly before reappearing a bit closer to the shore, swimming into the shallows and then making its way up onto the beach.

"Hello there," Bronwyn called out. Unsurprisingly there was no response, nothing more than a passing glance as it went about its business.

She sat there for a bit, watching the seal for as long as the light would allow before losing it in the darkness. She lit her candle as the sun finished its descent, marking time for her to leave.

She woke up the next morning and, just like any other day, made her way to the shop. Today was different though: today the door was already open and a familiar face was waiting for her.

"Owen!" She flung her arms around him as soon as he was close enough to do so. "I wasn't expecting you back so soon!"

"We decided to come back early. I have some good news to tell you. The shop will have to open a little late today."

"No need; I'm sure Finn will be happy to cover for me," said Bronwyn. "He owes me a favour and he's done it before."

"Owes you a favour, huh? He'd do anything you ask of him. Go fetch him, then. Meet me at the ship?"

"Finn's a good friend like that," Bronwyn muttered as she turned to leave. Her brother had only been back a few minutes and already he was getting on her nerves. But she did as he asked, installing Finn in the shop with promises to return from the docks as soon as she could.

Once at the ship it became abundantly clear what the good news was.

"Bronwyn, I would like to introduce you to my wife, Alys."

Bronwyn's face betrayed her surprise, but she quickly rearranged her features and did her best to be as welcoming as she could. Owen had been at sea for months so some changes were to be expected; this was more than she had prepared for, though.

Thankfully the social niceties couldn't last for long as there was work that needed doing – and Alys needed to go and see her new home – so Bronwyn excused herself and returned to the shop. Owen joined her a couple of hours later. Having had more time to process things, her congratulations this time were far more sincere, if cut a little short by Owen, bossy and brisk as usual.

"I've forgotten some important paperwork and need you to pick it up from the house for me. There are people coming to meet me here so I'll mind the shop while you're gone."

He explained what documents he needed and where to find them and before long Bronwyn found herself outside his – now also Alys's – home. Last time he was ashore she wouldn't have thought twice about walking straight in, but things had changed. She knocked on the door and waited. Her brother's instructions floated through her head but she was hesitant to act on them. It felt rude, intrusive. He had stressed some urgency, though, so after a minute she pushed through the reluctance and pushed the door open.

"Hello?" she called out, unable to bring herself to cross the threshold.

"Bronwyn?" a shaky voice responded. "Is that you? Come in."

"Owen said I could ..." Bronwyn started, stepping into the hallway as Alys came forward, the salt tracks of tears clearly visible on each cheek. "Is everything alright?"

"Of course, I'm just ... a little homesick." Alys shrugged, awkwardly wiping her face with the back of a hand. "Come in; there's no need to linger."

Bronwyn obliged, closing the door behind her before explaining, "Owen asked me to pick up some contracts for him. He's in a hurry for them ahead of some business meetings he has lined up. He's given me the key for the trunk."

"In that case I shan't offer you any tea," said Alys, smiling. "Sounds like you're in a hurry. I'm learning that when Owen wants something, he wants it now." She let out a brittle laugh. "I'll let you get on – but call if you need me."

Bronwyn's apprehension grew as she made her way to her brother's office and towards the chest he'd described. She didn't know Alys but she couldn't escape the feeling that it was something more than straightforward homesickness that ailed the girl. She also couldn't escape the knowledge that it was none of her business.

Fishing the key out of her apron, she crouched down and unlocked the trunk. It was well organised but almost full. Finding the paperwork required more rummaging than she was particularly comfortable with, even going as far as removing a sealskin cloak. It felt sturdy but she was tentative with it nonetheless, placing it on the floor as respectfully as she could while she fished out the locked metal document box beneath it, and offering it the same courtesy as she put it back and closed the lid. As she was locking up, she noticed a figure in the doorway.

"Did you find them okay?" Alys asked, hovering nervously in the doorway.

"Yes, thank you. Though hopefully he won't ask me to do this again. I always hate going through other people's things."

"Well, you'd best get going. Don't want to make him wait any longer than necessary."

"Are you going to be alright? You seem a little …" Bronwyn couldn't find the right word so she settled with standing up and straightening out her skirts instead.

"I'll be fine. I always am." Alys's words hung in the air as they stood there, neither really sure of what to say next but both knowing that something more was needed.

Alys broke the moment by turning away suddenly, gesturing for Bronwyn to follow her through the hallway to the door. She opened it and stood back.

"Some other time – for tea, perhaps." Another forced smile flitted across her face.

"Most days, after work, I head over to the beach for a while," said Bronwyn, on impulse. "You're welcome to join me if you wish."

"Oh, I wouldn't want to intrude on your time."

"You wouldn't be; Owen used to come but he's so busy these days. It would be nice to have some company again," said Bronwyn. "I'll be at the shop for the next couple of hours, so if you change your mind you know where to find me."

And with that she left. She didn't want to force the topic any more than she already had. But the longer she thought about it, the stronger the feeling that something was just not right with her brother and his new wife.

The rest of the work day was slow. Owen joined her near the end of it which helped the time pass somewhat. It was quieter than normal so a great opportunity for them to catch up. He told her the tales of his trip up north and the business plans he'd returned with. In turn, she filled him in on the local gossip, making sure to mention the invitation she'd extended to Alys, which he seemed pleased about. As nice as it was to spend time with her brother, Bronwyn found her anxiety increasing as closing time came around. Would Alys show up? Or would she view the offer as pity or something worse?

There was no sign of Alys by locking-up time. Part of Bronwyn's route aligned with Owen's walk home, so they kept each other company in silence as her anxiety turned to sadness. The rejection sat heavy in her heart and the relief she felt was visible as Alys rounded the corner ahead of them.

"I hope it's not too late to join you?"

"Not at all, I'm glad you could make it."

"You girls have fun, I'll see you later," Owen said as they'd reached the point where their paths diverged. He reached out to kiss Alys, and was offered a cheek. Bronwyn noticed her grimace switch to a smile as he stepped back and left them to it.

The women made their way along the coastline, passing by plenty of perfectly good spots before finally reaching Bronwyn's preferred area.

"Why here?" Alys asked.

"Our sister used to bring us here. It was her spot. Now it's mine." Bronwyn replied as she settled into the sand, Alys quickly following suit.

"Owen didn't tell me he has two sisters."

"Had. It's a sensitive topic for him. For us."

"I'm so sorry; I had no idea," said Alys, her eyes swimming with fresh tears.

"If you're to be a part of this family then it's a story worth knowing. Though some other time perhaps."

"No, please, tell me more about her; what was she like?"

Bronwyn obliged and, once started, the conversation flowed with ease. Any initial awkwardness between them was gone as they relaxed in each other's company.

This quickly became a routine. Alys would meet Bronwyn at the shop and together they'd walk to the beach and watch the sunset – or the sky darken when that was all the weather would allow.

Each time they opened up just a little bit more, first just sharing easy stories, then reminiscing about times gone by, and eventually Bronwyn felt brave enough to broach a more personal topic.

"Is everything okay?"

"Why wouldn't it be?"

"You've been here for a few months now and I don't think I've seen you look genuinely happy since you arrived."

"I've enjoyed our time together; does that not count?"

"No; I've enjoyed it too but there's always this tinge of sadness hanging over you."

"I'm sorry."

"It's not something to apologise for. If you're not happy, then why stay?"

They sat in silence for a while, the weight of the conversation lingering over them both. But Bronwyn had resolved to get to the bottom of the matter.

"Alys? Talk to me, please."

And she did. Everything Alys had been keeping to herself poured out and finally Bronwyn understood. And she knew what she needed to do.

"Wait right here; I'll be back."

There was no response when she knocked on their door, so she let herself in and made her way to Owen's office. She lifted the sash on the window before doing anything else, then picked up a poker from the fireplace and crossed the room to the trunk. It took some effort but she managed to lever the padlock off the lid, remembering what Finn had told her when helping with security at the shop: a lock is only as strong as the screws that hold it in place.

With the cloak in hand, she bolted out of the window, just as the sound of the front door opening reached her.

Her escape was by no means graceful, but it was efficient. She was out and away with her haul and halfway down the street before Owen's shouts could be heard. She sprinted for as long as her body – and her skirts – would allow, slowing to a jog as she reached an open stretch of the path. But the respite did not last long: Owen was following, and fast. She picked up the pace once more.

She refused to look back. It didn't matter how close he was, all that mattered was reaching Alys and before she knew it the cove was upon her. As the path descended to the beach, Bronwyn barely slowed. The path was slippery and uneven, but she knew it better than Owen, so it was a risk she was comfortable taking.

Alys was sitting just where she had left her, gazing out to sea. Bronwyn launched herself down the beach towards her friend, the glimpse of Owen painfully close behind her. He always was the faster of them.

"Go!" She threw the cloak and grabbed her brother, who was reaching for Alys, putting all her weight into unbalancing him. She hit the sand hard but didn't care; he was there beside her and her goal had been achieved.

Bronwyn looked up just in time to see Alys standing in the waves, the edges of the cloak whipping in the wind as she wrapped it around her body. As she did so, the wind ceased to have any effect on it. It moulded to her skin and then transformed, sleek and glossy, as she lifted the hood over her head and bent forwards. No longer confined to human form, she slipped under the waves and left them behind without so much as a second glance.

The sun gently kissed the horizon as it began its embrace with the depths. Two seal heads popped out of the water, breaking the surface as they came up for air. They dipped back under briefly before reappearing a bit closer to the shore. One of them stayed put while the other swam into the shallows and walked up the beach to Bronwyn. She folded the cloak over her arm as she neared.

"Alys. You came back."

"Don't sound so surprised." She sat down next to Bronwyn, closer than she had dared to before.

"You left. I thought …" Her voice caught in her throat as Alys gently rested her head on her shoulder.

"You thought I wouldn't even say goodbye?"

"Is that what this is? Goodbye?"

"If you wish."

"No!"

"Well … You could come with me, perhaps?"

"I think I would like that."

Partings
Pamela Vass

A Mother's Parting

Her hands seek a familiar grip on the back of the chair, the linen antimacassar grubby now to younger eyes but still as crisp and new to Eva as the day she lifted it from her bottom drawer. Agitated fingers move down to pluck at the well-worn arms, a comforting ritual as she shifts back and forth from then to now, now to then, then to now, no then … much better.

When there were no strangers taking clothes from her wardrobe, lifting familiar images from the walls revealing oblongs and circles of pristine wallpaper, filling black bags with her life.

When there was no one to say what she could keep, what had to go: her mother's rug, Arthur's jacket from behind the kitchen door, the children's drawings on the pantry wall. Voices, hands, opinions, all poking into her life. Uninvited, unwanted, unhearing. She'd asked them politely to go, to leave her be. But her voice was lost the moment she missed the handle and tipped boiling water down her side.

This is her home. No time since she and Arthur ducked under the confetti shower as they left the chapel and ran down the lane to

Instow sands, just yards from their new front door. They walked through that door into a life that fitted perfectly, mirrored in Arthur's paintings on the walls and her mother's rug in pride of place on the parlour floor. So many happy hours side by side in their well-chosen chairs, protected with antimacassars proudly decorated with her handcrafted lace, shaped to their resting heads over the years.

She sits contentedly in her chair, knowing that as the days shorten the sun now setting behind Appledore church will soon disappear beyond the boatyard further down the estuary. And on the next high tide she will have a grandstand view of the float out when the latest hull emerges from the cavernous dockyard. With the changing season the delights of summer days on the beach, Hockings ice creams, grandchildren playing in the dunes, will fade. The smaller boats will soon be lifted by cranes, precariously balanced on the old quay, to winter in the boatyard. Sand will drift across the road, caught up in the first autumn gales. She shares the memories with Arthur, still present within these walls. He is in the coat she touches each time she closes the kitchen door, his paint brushes in the conservatory, his impression on the far side of the bed.

She wishes for more time in this chair, this place. Seeds sown in the community over years have born fruit as meals appeared when illness struck, invitations were given and returned, short strolls to the beach were rewarded with welcome conversations. More time sharing the comforting routine of chapel, followed by lunch at the Commodore with a personal greeting. More time with family and friends filling her home, moving seamlessly from hosting Christmas to birthdays, from farewells to new arrivals. Being known. Being home.

Home is where she is surrounded by photos, names kindly added by a lifelong friend: little nudges that help faces fall into place. Where rooms are navigated with ease, clothes and utensils found, routines followed without conscious thought, guided by years of comforting familiarity. Even with fading sight, the gentle rhythm of the same number of steps to the bathroom, down the stairs, to the kitchen, to the kettle ... to the boiling kettle.

So hands are now removing her fingers from the chair, guiding her arm into a heavy winter coat, her best coat, not to be worn on a Tuesday. What do they know? Already they are pressing her head down, bending her, folding her into the car, into a smaller life. The belt is tight around her chest, constraining her, containing her, all her life's rhythms suddenly gone.

A Son's Parting

He stares ahead, lacks the courage to meet his mother's eyes. He wants to shout, tell her to stop fidgeting with the belt, stop complaining about the house, stop moaning about the things that have gone, stop making it all his fault. She'd agreed, hadn't she? Eventually. Agreed that the last scalding was one too many.

He races the engine; guilty tension holds his foot on the pedal, his fury directed at the elderly driver too carefully reversing his Nissan Micra into his driveway. Didn't ought to be on the roads at his age.

She's quiet now. Veined, blotched hands still clutch at the belt, prising it away from her body, but she won't ask him to ease it. "Have meals on wheels," he'd said. But she wouldn't. "Have someone in to give you a bath," he'd said. But she wouldn't. What choice did he have?

Her hand grabs the door as the car bounces off the curb.

"Damn! Lost the bloody wheel trim now." A car horn blasts as he pulls up and hurls himself out of the door to retrieve it. It's spun down the bank, too far down – but he's past care or caution and is suddenly rolling, grasping at the earth, landing heavily.

Memories flash, rolling down this bank as a child with other boys bunking off from the village school. Foolish in this tiny community. Best to wait for the weekend, but when did nine-year-old boys ever postpone the thrill of mischief-making? And his mother, sneaking upstairs with cocoa and biscuits to his bedroom where his father had banished him before tea.

He smiles, recalling innocent pleasures. The lunchtime treats she brought to the ruined boat on the beach where they made camps, sailed the high seas and repelled pirates. His vigilance, guarding the biscuit tin as it slowly inched towards full with small change from random relations and a Saturday job delivering papers. And his delight when the brand new pound coins mysteriously started appearing: solved when he caught his mother quietly lifting the lid and dropping something inside.

The thrill, when finally he could walk through the gates of the boatyard to learn to sail the Lasers, Darts and Redwings that rested at the side of the estuary. Numerous capsizes failed to dent his mother's faith in him, faith repaid when he sailed her to Lundy. Together they had walked to Jenny's Cove and nestled into the hillside to watch the puffins, familiar patterns reversing now as she looked to him for shelter from the wind and a supportive arm across the tussocks.

He looks back at the car. His mother has managed to release the seat belt and is standing at the top of the slope.

"Oh no!" Her agitated voice reaches him. "All those flowers; those beautiful flowers." She kneels heavily on the ground and cradles the crushed petals in her hands. "So much life." Her tears fall. "Gone, all gone."

The Split: Before and After
Damien Mansfield

The Walker slowed and looked for a place to sit. Casting about, she spotted a fallen tree in just the right place to see the entirety of Bideford bay: a beautiful view originally but today it just brought back memories of that night. She slipped her pack off, eased herself down onto the trunk and stretched her braced leg out, a grimace of pain and relief crossing her face.

Westward Ho! She'd left this village four years ago with no plans to return – not in this lifetime anyway. The devastation left by the split had almost levelled it and the encroaching sea hadn't done this formerly lovely village much good. A small laugh escaped as she smiled for the first time in weeks and contemplated the remains of the various blocks of flats that had been erected in her childhood years. "Silver lining there," she whispered. Even with nobody in sight, speaking aloud was now so alien to her that a whisper was the loudest vocalisation she felt comfortable uttering.

As she stared down at the collapsed buildings and rusted cars, the sounds of pulverising masonry, screaming metal (and people but that sound was quashed) started to steal into her mind. The Walker felt her balance shift at the memory of feeling the earth move under her feet as she fled with the first wave of refugees, glancing left to see waves rearing up many times higher than the sea wall. Her chest tightened as she slipped from the fallen trunk and sprawled, eyes showing the whites all around, fighting the panic that burnt those memories across her mind. She wasn't aware of the scream that tore itself out of her body, nor was she aware of the murder of crows that lifted from the derelict houses lining Cornborough Road at the sudden explosion of sound. Her mind shut down the conscious part, letting the memories become nightmares, dreams, blankness.

When the Walker came back, she noted that the sun was in a significantly different place, less than a hand's width above the horizon, and streaking the sea with lines of fire. Lundy Islands were thrown into sharp relief, highlighting the valley that now separated them. With a groan, she pulled herself up. She sat back on her tree and looked down the much steeper hill towards Nelson Road and her former home. At the moment, her old bungalow was invisible under water. She realised there wasn't much chance of visiting that little bungalow today. Maybe later, at low tide, whatever low tide meant now.

Cursing herself for letting the day get away from her, she pulled her pack open and began the process of setting up camp. The verge at the top of Stanwell Hill had overgrown in the intervening time but she preferred that: less chance of discovery. Her tent was a small dome, just big enough for the Walker and her pack. When home was properly set up, she built a small fire inside high banks to stop light spillage. She unwrapped the squirrel she had trapped and skinned the day before, spitted it and set it over the fire. As it cooked she looked through the meagre supply of books she had salvaged, before deciding to revisit Stephen King. She briefly wondered if he had survived and hurriedly shut that line of questioning down. One episode was quite enough, thank you. After dinner had been eaten, the book reluctantly put away and night had fallen, she crawled into her tent, unstrapped her leg and took one last look at the shattered moon. With a shudder, she pulled the flaps closed and settled down to whatever sleep she could get.

To sleep, and remember ...

The dreams came in a series of flash frames, each image disappearing as soon as it appeared.

I'm six, playing on the green and watching the framework of yet another set of flats taking form. Images of school, friends, parties, happiness and squabbles ...

I'm eleven, just starting my time at Bideford College. Skip to the end ...

Eighteen and leaving college with surprisingly good grades ...

Starting my first job as a carer; advancing and running my own care home by thirty. A good career ...

The year 2040: the start of the lunar mining project. Live streams from the surface, astronauts conducting virtual tours, bouncing around and hitting golf balls. The first drilling, rock dust billowing and the cheers over the helmet radios as they officially begin mining ...

Later in 2042: the live streams fragmenting and cutting off in the early evening. News reports of contact being lost after a moonquake started. Going outside, looking up and seeing the moon splitting into two, three, four, too many pieces to count. Realisation hitting. Running inside, dragging out my old blue frame hiking pack and getting ready to go ...

Two days later and the shock wave arriving. Four in the morning, the earth moving. Diving out of bed, dragging on clothes, boots, pack and running. I forgot to lock— Screw it! Running, part of the herd. Waves, insanely large ones, hitting the sea wall and not stopping. Getting uphill, barely ahead of the water. People falling, too slow, pulled back into the maelstrom that was her home village. Babble falling from lips: prayers, pleas, cries of panic and bargaining. Safety, looking down on boiling waters, the ground shuddering and bucking. Less people, sounds of pain, suffering and unrestrained grief. The realisation that the world would never be the same. Ever.

Every day, for the next couple of years, followed pretty much the same pattern of wandering around trying to find other people, looting shops that had been abandoned and subsisting a day at a time ...

Oh god, not this dream again.

Travelling across Dartmoor, hoping people had travelled south to warmer climes. Stepping on that dirt clod that hid the animal trap, hearing my leg snap before the pain hit me. The trapper looking after me – and thankfully knowing some medicine. Didn't hurt that he was quite cute too. Four months as the leg heals but it will never be perfect again. We built my brace together and I still use the Mk V version. He helped me learn to walk again, taught me how to trap and set snares so I could eat. This was a pleasant time but we both knew it would end. I would resume wandering even though it was very nice having companionship and ... well ... I'm only human ...

Leaving the trapper and resuming wandering, heading northeast this time, aiming for Taunton and further into the country. Reaching the divide. Realising no help is coming if this new sea channel hasn't been bridged yet. Turning back to explore and wander. The farm, not sure where but probably North Devon. The man in chains. The farmer raising his shotgun. The blast—

The Walker awoke, sitting rigidly upright, the blast of the shotgun still ringing in her ears. Knowing she would get no more sleep, she shuffled to the tent flaps and tied them open so she could watch the sky. Glumly, she stared at the shattered moon and thought of the time in not so may years when some of those fragments would be coming home with a bang. As always, she prayed the shards were not shedding their light on her when they did. As the sun rose, casting light down Bayview Road to warm her, the Walker stretched and began her morning rituals. She grinned as she looked for a bush without many thorns, thinking how some habits died hard.

After finishing off the squirrel, re-packing and re-strapping, the Walker started the steep walk into the village proper. The road was cracked and rippled in places but she had walked over worse terrain in the last ... three years? Four? She couldn't remember exactly and didn't feel like expending the energy to work it out right now. As she descended, she looked around, noticing how nature was reclaiming the hillside. Saplings had sprouted from the spaces – and even trunks – of fallen brethren and grass was already well established in the gaping cracks of the road surface. The day was chilly for August and the Walker thanked her sleeping bag for its warmth and allowing her to wake up without stiff joints.

As the Walker reached the bottom of the hill she saw that the way was blocked by a mix of rubble, fallen trees and new growth. Groaning at the difficulty she envisioned, she clambered, wriggled and slipped over and through the blockage, frequently having to turn back for a better route and cursing when branches or thorns caught her clothing or brace – and cursing louder when they found skin to scratch and pierce. Eventually she found herself standing atop a small hillock at the top of Nelson Road. She surveyed the scene before her, noting that the tide had receded slightly but she would still need to wade past her former home. With a sigh, she hitched up her backpack and began walking again. She had been hoping the water would recede further overnight so that she could look through the shops closer to the sea wall. It didn't seem likely as she could see a high-water mark halfway up a fragment of the church wall that had survived at the bottom of Lakenham Hill.

As she drew near her house the water drew up to her knees, then past, making the Walker gasp and giggle slightly as she remembered old times at the beach, walking in slowly to get used to the water temperature and then all her careful work being negated by breakers soaking her from head to foot. Luckily, no waves were in evidence and she was able to acclimatise at her own pace today.

She drew level with her old house, looking down into the rock pool it had become. True, the rocks were masonry from the new flats next door but the effect was the same. She laughed out loud when she noticed that while the new flats had become more literal in their naming, her 100-odd-year-old stone bungalow was still basically intact. The laugh echoed back and forth along the street and she clamped a hand over her mouth. That was the loudest sound she had made in, what, a year? Maybe more.

Moving away from the remains of her former life, she set her sights on the stores along the street. Going along Golf Links Road was out: the shops would be flooded and she had no interest in swimming into one. The Walker knew that she would likely find very little of use but hope springs eternal when you're trying to survive. She briefly wondered why nobody had returned to re-settle the dryer parts of the village. The universe, being in a providing mood today, provided the answer in short order.

As the Walker drew level with the tackle shop, she briefly toyed with idea of making camp, grabbing one of the rods from what was left of the window display and catching some fish – a welcome change in diet – when a sound froze her in place. It wasn't a loud sound but it was a sound that had signalled danger to man for thousands of years. A growl: long, low and constant. It was a warning and a promise, both of pain and death. Spinning around, the Walker found the source in a thin, mangy dog slowly padding out of the empty doorway of the shop on the corner ahead of her.

She began to back away slowly, eyes darting this way and that for a stone ... something ... anything that she could throw and scare the dog away. She thought fleetingly of the machete strapped to her backpack, dismissing it immediately as the very, VERY last resort. A shifting of glass pulled her attention back to the doorway and her mind screamed at what she saw. A pack at least ten strong was following the first dog. Eighteen eyes and four empty sockets fixed on her form as she retreated. Courtesy of millions of years of evolution, her bladder let go as she dropped all pretence and ran back the way she had come, splashing deeper into the water and hoping they wouldn't follow. No such luck: these dogs obviously liked baths. She angled back across the road, heading for the rubble next to her old home. Reaching it, the Walker pulled herself up onto the pile and began liberating rocks she could use. She turned and yelled down at the dogs, "Bad dogs! Go home! Go on, get out of here!"

Naturally, this had no effect and she threw her first rock, aiming it in front of the pack leader. As it splashed down, he leader merely shifted his course. She tried again, several times, but the dog kept coming. Grinding her teeth and asking forgiveness, she selected a small rock and aimed directly at the closest dog. The stone glanced off its nose, eliciting a yelp and a sudden confusion under the water as the dog back-pedalled. A few more rocks, close enough to splash but not hit, convinced the leader that this meal was more trouble that it was worth. The pack turned and paddled back to the edge of the water.

The leader turned, shook itself and fixed her with a long stare. Message received. Westward Ho! was not a place she was welcome any longer. The Walker stayed put until the pack had returned to the shop then followed with a few rocks. She bounced a few off the doorway they had used, just as insurance, and continued her walk up Atlantic Way and out of her home.

Around lunchtime, the Walker arrived at her next port of call: Bideford, a town she had loved to visit in the past. After the big shopping complex had gone bust, the council regeneration initiative had brought shops back to town. Most of the new ones had been family owned, the sort not seen in town for fifteen years before that day. Today though, her attention was on the hills across the river. Smoke trails were rising over Pollyfield Park. Smoke meant fires, and fires meant people. The bridge was unusable, being ten feet underwater but she found row-boats tethered in the high street. She eagerly clambered into one, ready to meet people again.

A few minutes later, the bow of the boat crunched against the edge of a landing stage built in the train station. She cursed her terrible rowing, tied up and began the walk to the park. She passed a tent, then a small cluster of tents, with curious faces cautiously peeping out … more up ahead. Rows of tents! She walked slowly through them, trying to project calm and friendliness. A woman came to meet her, the air of authority identifying her as the leader. The Walker stopped and raised a hand in greeting as she thought about what to say.

Her voice croaked at the first attempt.

The woman smiled and the Walker swallowed and tried again.

"Hi there."

The Kelpie
Lalla Merlin

Lucy Jarret was nasty. She was the type of person to kick a puppy. I know: she kicked mine when she thought I wasn't looking. We were in the same form at school and went to the same riding school on Saturdays, so there was no escaping her. Everyone hated and feared her, except adults – teachers especially. They seemed to have a blind spot as far as Lucy was concerned.

Lucy was horrible to everyone, but she seemed to hate me especially, calling me 'the witch'. Perhaps it was because of my gipsy looks: I had inherited the dark hair and bright eyes of my Romany ancestors from my grandmother. Gran had been one of the few adults who wasn't charmed by Lucy. A nasty piece of work, she had called her.

Ponies were the only thing Lucy and I had in common, though neither of us was likely to own one. She lived at the edge of the village with a garden not much bigger than a postage stamp. We had a field, but it was useless for a pony: a stream ran through it; most of it was marsh and the rest was mud. The only corner that was usable was occupied by ancient Cully, Gran's old piebald, dreaming away his final days in the shade of the trees. I used to stand with him sometimes, gazing over the marsh and dreaming of ponies while the puppy dug madly in the mud.

Lucy made my life a misery at school, and managed to torment me even at the stables. She would tack up the ponies and make sure my pony's girth was twisted or my stirrup leathers the wrong length. Or she'd ride alongside me on a hack, taunting me. "I bet you can't jump that fallen log," she'd say, knowing I couldn't. Then she'd put her pony over it easily. That was the other thing, you see. She was a far better rider than I'd ever be. It wasn't fair.

"Ignore her," Mum said. "She can't be that bad, surely."

Gran would have understood, but Gran was dead. I had inherited, among other things, her books. Sometimes I read them, just to feel close to her, those strange tales full of old magic. They should have been burnt, really, along with everything else in her brightly painted wagon, as was traditional among her people – but I had rescued them.

One day Lucy went too far. When she tacked up the ponies she shoved a thorn under my saddle so my pony went nuts, bucking and twisting to relieve the pain, and I fell off, humiliatingly, in front of everyone.

"You should stick to riding a broomstick," Lucy told me. "Leave ponies to people who understand them."

At home I went straight to Gran's oldest book, which was bound in cracked, black leather and, following its instructions, I collected herbs and I dropped them in the stream that crossed the marsh meadow, while murmuring the strange words. In my head Gran frowned, the long white-streaked hair falling down around her dark face. "No good will come of a wish like that," she warned.

But I wasn't after something good.

I phoned Lucy.

I told her, "My parents have bought me a pony. I bet you can't make him jump over the stream in our field." I put the phone away.

The kelpie was standing in the stream in the shape of a black pony, its mane and tail streaming with water. As it heard me approach it swung its head, and for a moment mad shark-eyes glared at me from a pony's face. Then its transformation was complete. It wrenched itself from the stream bed, whinnied softly and trotted towards me: the gentlest, sweetest pony, wearing a bridle of green leather and no saddle at all. I patted its neck, noticing the slight stickiness, and it nudged at my arm invitingly. Ride me, it seemed to say.

'A kelpie's coat has glue-like qualities. If you mount it you will be unable to dismount, and the kelpie will gallop to the nearest river or stream and dive in, carrying you to a watery world where it will devour you.'

I undid the throat lash of the green bridle.

'The power of a kelpie is contained in its bridle. With the bridle in your possession, it is yours to command.'

The pony threw up its head, and something un-pony-like looked out of its eyes, but I drew the bridle off and tucked it under my jacket. "There's your victim," I told it, nodding towards the gate over which Lucy was climbing. The puppy saw Lucy and rushed over to greet her. Lucy kicked out at him, and he bowled over on the grass, yelping.

The kelpie whickered gently as Lucy reached us, and she looked at it critically.

"Not bad," she remarked. "What a waste. Don't your parents realise you're a useless rider?"

I bent over and picked up the puppy, which had limped to me for comfort.

"Bet you can't ride my pony," I taunted Lucy. "Without tack. Bet you can't jump him over the stream."

Lucy looked at the stream, narrow between its marshy banks.

"Of course I can," she said.

"Go on, then." I stroked the puppy's ears, and it licked my hand.

Lucy vaulted onto the kelpie, and it turned towards the stream, ears pricked. Lucy kicked it, harder than necessary. In the distance, Cully lifted his head and watched through clouded eyes.

The kelpie neighed and began to canter towards the stream, transforming before my eyes. Scales replaced the black coat; knife-sharp teeth flashed and shark-eyes glared as the canter changed to a gallop and it leapt into the air then plunged, Lucy and all, into the stream that shouldn't have been deep enough to take them but somehow was. They disappeared beneath the surface and Lucy's astonished shriek hung for a moment on the evening air, then faded and was gone. In the distance old Cully dropped his head and began to graze.

I picked up the puppy, mud and all, kissed him on the head, and wandered towards home.

Miss Emily Eden
Lalla Merlin

"Look ..." The boy's father was pointing to the old photograph hanging on the school wall, one in a row stretching far into the past, where boys with short-back-and-sides haircuts and girls with tight plaits squinted into a sun that had set over sixty years ago. This photograph was more recent, though its colours had faded into pastels. He spoke in a reminiscent tone. "The school was much smaller then; only two classes of twenty children, and two teachers."

Toby fidgeted, jumping up for a closer look. "When was this, Dad? A hundred years ago?"

His father, Alan, laughed. "No. But a long time: nearly thirty years ago. Look closely: is there anyone you recognise?" The child frowned in concentration. Alan lifted him for a closer look, but he squirmed free. "Dad! One of my friends might see! I'm five years old, you know!"

His mother distracted him, pointing at the picture. "Look, Toby. What about that boy with the sticking-up hair?"

Toby peered, then crowed, "You, Dad! It looks like you!"

Alan laughed. "It is me... This was my school. I lived in Devon when I was a boy."

Toby continued to scrutinise the photograph. "You had lots more hair then, Dad."

His father passed a hand ruefully over his receding hairline. "It brought me a lot of trouble. It wouldn't lie down no matter how often I brushed it. The headmaster was convinced I made it stick up on purpose."

"My head teacher lets us have our hair however we want it," Toby told him smugly. Then, pointing at a looming figure in the picture, "Who's that?"

His father shuddered involuntarily, then made a joke of it. "That man walked in my nightmares: Mr. Beahan, the headmaster. He was about ten feet tall and terrifying."

Alan's wife, Becky, had noticed his instinctive response and squeezed his hand comfortingly. Toby was still engrossed in the photograph. "And who's that?" 'That' was a timid-looking woman with grey hair and a singularly mischievous smile. She was holding one tiny child's hand unobtrusively, and had her arm round another.

Toby's father sighed. "Ah. The love of my life. Miss Emily Eden. She was our protector against the Awful Headmaster. He bullied her terribly. I always swore I'd come back one day as a knight on a great white charger and rescue her."

"You wanted to be a knight? On a horse?" Toby was scornful. "Why not an Avenger? Or Dr Who in the TARDIS? Then she could have been your companion. She looks a bit old, though." Outside, a megaphone squawked incomprehensibly.

"She wasn't that old," Toby's father told him defensively.

Becky laughed. "Come on, Toby. It sounds as if sports day is beginning. You need to go and put on your running shoes, and Daddy and I need to find seats."

Outside, the sun was dazzling. Parents arranged themselves and their picnics in groups on the parched grass. Stalls were set up round the edges of the field, a barbeque sent acrid smoke into the still air and an ice-cream van was doing a roaring trade. Alan and Becky settled themselves on a rug. Becky opened the hamper and poured them both chilled drinks. "What's the first race?" she asked, reaching for the programme. "Goodness, do you realise there are seven year groups divided into girls and boys, and all of them run about five races. That's ... let me see ... seventy races! We'll be here for hours!' Alan drained his spritzer, before holding out his glass for more. "Steady!" Becky told him. She studied his face for a second. "Alan? What's the matter?"

He shrugged. "I'm sorry. This is the first sports day I've been to since I was a child. I loathed sports day. It was nothing like this, of course, but it was held right here. It was the headmaster's hobbyhorse: he drilled us for it all year, making our lives a misery with his stopwatch. He should have been an army drill sergeant, not a teacher. That's what Miss Eden said, anyway. She made things bearable, somehow. She turned Mr B into a sort of bad joke. She hated sports day, too. I think she'd have sabotaged it if she dared."

Becky refilled his glass. "Well, don't let the ghost of a dead headmaster spoil today for you – or for any of us. Toby's so thrilled you're here to watch him."

Alan grinned. "I'll enter into the spirit of it, I promise. And I won't let the old bully haunt me. Miss Emily Eden wouldn't have approved of that at all."

A megaphone boomed. Children who had been milling around under the chestnut tree at the far side of the field, lined up at the starting line, balancing potatoes on spoons.

"Potatoes?" Alan asked, mystified. "Isn't this billed as an egg-and-spoon race?"

Becky nodded. "I don't suppose they're allowed to use real eggs anymore because of salmonella, or something. Look, there's Toby. Toby!" she called, cupping her hands round her mouth. Toby waved enthusiastically from the starting line and dropped his potato. Retrieving it, he replaced it on the spoon, holding it firmly in place with a thumb.

The race was on. Five-year-olds trundled down the track, eyes unwaveringly on their potatoes, tongues between teeth in concentration. A boy tripped, his potato flew some distance, his face crumpled – and from nowhere a small dog appeared, erupting onto the track at speed and making off with the potato. It tore round in circles before dropping the potato in front of the little boy, who was climbing to his feet, then chased its tail ludicrously. The boy, who had been on the brink of tears, grinned and set off in pursuit of his competitors, several of whom had paused to watch the antics of the dog, which was now trotting at the little boy's heels. A ripple of laughter ran round the field, then applause broke out: the first child had crossed the finishing line.

"Look!" Becky cried, "It's Toby!" She clapped frantically. Toby, clutching a rosette, beamed vaguely in their direction, but seemed far more interested in the dog, now begging by the barbeque stall.

"Do you think he should have been holding the potato onto the spoon so firmly?" Alan asked.

A woman sitting on a rug near theirs smiled across. "Oh, nobody minds that sort of thing," she said. "They don't mean to cheat. Anyway, it would be a pity to take sports day too seriously, wouldn't it?"

"Absolutely," Alan agreed with conviction. "Look – the dog's at it again!"

A girls' potato-and-spoon race was now under way, and the dog was joining in with gusto, tearing up and down the track barking, then pausing to scratch an ear or roll on the ground, wriggling ecstatically. The children were enchanted, forgetting their race in their efforts to stroke and pat the dog. Clearly wary of being caught and having its fun curtailed, the dog dodged effortlessly, earning applause from delighted spectators and groans of frustration from the children.

Race followed race, and the dog joined in every one, undermining any competitive spirit and creating an atmosphere of hilarity. Any child who seemed to be losing their sense of humour was a target for the dog's antics. She rolled, dug holes in the track and chased her tail, bringing a grin to the face of the most determined prize-seeker.

"Whose dog is that?" Alan asked at last.

The woman next to them glanced across. "This is your first sports day here?"

"Well—" Alan began.

"Yes," Becky agreed.

The woman continued, "This is my sixth – my daughter is in the top class – and as long as I have been coming, that dog has been joining in. Nobody knows who she belongs to, and nobody has ever been able to catch her. She has become something of a school legend. Look at the school logo."

Becky flipped the programme over, revealing the familiar logo: a string of children running after a small dog. "Oh!" she exclaimed: "I thought it represented the spirit of childhood – I didn't realise it referred to an actual dog!"

"A series of dogs, probably," the woman corrected. "The same logo – with variations – has been used for over twenty years. The theory is that there's a family of farm terriers that passes a fondness for sports day from mother to daughter."

Alan laughed. "It sounds pretty unlikely," he said.

"True," the woman agreed. "But so does a dog that attends school sports days for twenty years."

The last race was run, prizes were awarded – Toby received a certificate to put on his wall, which delighted him – and the children were free to join their parents and explore the sideshows. There was a queue for the bouncy castle, and every small hand seemed to be clutching an ice cream. Reaching the front of the queue at the hot-dog stall, Alan felt a nudge at his ankle. Glancing down, he saw the terrier panting up at him, tongue lolling and stumpy tail wagging frantically.

"Get her a hot dog, Dad," Toby begged.

"A hot dog for a hot dog?" Alan asked. "Why not. Four hot dogs, please." He glanced down at the dog. "Onions? Mustard?" The dog sneezed. "Um, one without onions or mustard." The dog followed them back to their rug and took the hot dog delicately from Alan's hand.

Their neighbour smiled. "I've never seen her let anyone get so close," she remarked. Alan stroked the dog's head, and it paused in its dissection of the sausage to lick his hand briefly. The woman leant over to give it a pat but the dog leapt to its feet and dodged. The woman laughed. "You are honoured."

"Animal magnetism," said Alan. "Look – they're drawing the raffle." The dog finished its sausage and tore off across the field with Toby in laughing pursuit, collecting a string of children and re-creating the school logo against the sun-soaked evening while Alan and Becky moved closer to the raffle.

"Number 332: that's us!" Becky hissed. "Go and collect the prize!" Alan shoved his way politely through the crowd of bodies and returned, slightly pink around the ears, carrying a ludicrously oversized bouquet.

"Goodness," Becky remarked mildly, "I don't think we've got a vase big enough."

"Never mind," Toby said, reappearing at her elbow and fidgeting pointedly with his rosette. "It's nice to win, isn't it, Mum?" He yawned.

"Come on," Alan said, scooping him up, "It's time we went home." They said their farewells and made their way to the school car park.

Fishing the car keys from her bag, Becky paused. "Look," she said. "There's the dog. She must be going home, too." The little terrier had emerged from the school field and was trotting purposefully up the lane. At the corner she turned and looked back towards them, wagging her stump of a tail.

Toby wriggled out of his father's arms. "Let's see where she goes!" he said.

Becky hesitated. "Why not. Come on, then: let's solve this mystery!"

Holding hands, Toby in the middle, they followed the dog. She led them into the centre of the village, then turned through a gateway.

"Is it the farm where she lives?" asked Toby.

"No," Alan replied. "It's the churchyard. Must be a shortcut."

The dog led them briskly past ancient, leaning tombstones almost hidden among long grass and wild poppies, round the corner of the church to a tidier area where the grass was trimmed and the headstones all a uniform polished granite with black lettering. Then she leapt onto a raised grave and curled up to wait for them, her button eyes bright.

Toby stumbled. "Carry me, Mum," he said plaintively. "I'm tired from winning my race."

"I'll carry you," Alan said.

"No, I want Mum," insisted Toby. Becky lifted him, and he rested his cheek on her shoulder briefly. "Where has the dog gone?" he asked.

"Um ... I don't know," Becky replied. "She was on one of the graves. She must have slipped off home. Now, which grave was it?"

"It was this one," Alan said softly. He was reading the words on the headstone. He bent and placed the raffle-prize bouquet on the grave. "Let's get back to the car," he said. "It's growing chilly." Slowly, they retraced their steps.

"It's been a lovely day, hasn't it?" Toby said sleepily.

"Yes," Alan agreed. "It was by far the best sports day I have ever been to."

Their voices faded, and their footfalls. In the churchyard the shadows lengthened slowly and a bee bumbled round the enormous bouquet marking the grave of Miss Emily Eden.

Pickled Cockles
Jade Ruby

Gingerly, I step forward and immediately wince as the coldness seeps in through the holes in my rubber shoes. I slip slightly on something slimy underfoot.

"Urgh!" I cry, looking up wretchedly as an island of seaweed leans chummily against my waist.

"The best ones are just past those rocks," Granny cries excitedly from her chair, where she sits resplendent in tartan wool and a beret. "Go across to that bit and you'll be able to reach."

I think longingly of the clifftop above, wondering how my little car is faring in the car park with my grumpy teenage daughter at the helm. There's no way I can turn back now though; I'm committed to this.

The sea is rolling further and further away, leaving behind a patchwork of stones in all shapes and sizes: some sharp and others worn smooth by years of rollicking waves and brutal undercurrents. Green algae coats the largest rocks and beneath them are the rock pools where tiny creatures are thriving. Soft sand and shingle beds house unique little universes of miniscule shrimp and creeping crabs shielded by gutweed and bladderwrack.

The deepest rock pool remains submerged, a large recess of saltwater that blocks my way from the sandy verge, the place where the cockles lie buried beneath. To get there, I have to cross this freezing patch of water. Not an easy task in the depths of winter.

"Why didn't you wear your boots and waders? That's far easier."

"Why didn't we go to Clovelly? That would have been far easier." I retort. "We could have bought what we need from the fishermen."

"It's not the same!" Granny snorts. I'm reminded of the beach's namesake. As if spiritually connected, Grace suddenly appears beside her. "Do you know, Mum." She calls to me, her long hair whipping wildly in the wind beneath her bobble hat. "This is called Grunta Beach on account of some pigs that were stranded here after their boat was shipwrecked? How funny is that? The noise must have been crazy."

"Hilarious." I mutter, folding my arms across my shivering frame. My tattered swimming costume looks extremely bleak, even more so up against my daughter's thick coat.

"Did you lock the car?" I ask sternly, playing for time. I'm rewarded with an eye roll, which seemingly conveys the affirmative. She is only fourteen, but on the cusp of adulthood. She sometimes catches me unawares with the side profile of her elegant face. It takes my breath away when she's suddenly the image of the woman she will become. Right now, she prefers reading to rap music yet still wouldn't be caught dead hanging out with her boring old mother and funny little sister. She'll make an exception for Granny, but today she'd much rather get lost in a novel and put her feet up on the dashboard of my car, her sanctuary during this trip.

Wrapped up against the elements in bright waterproofs, my nine-year-old, Norah, is busying herself in a shallow rock pool close to Granny's camping chair. Her pink bucket is a fairy pond decorated with her favourite finds: the left-behind shells of limpets, mussels and velvet swimming crabs. I see her inspect a mermaid's purse before plopping that inside, too. Her fingers delicately trace each treasure, memorising the texture and pattern of every item. Her strawberry-blonde hair is clumped with saltwater from bending down to reach for more gems.

"Don't dawdle!" Granny calls to me. "If it wasn't for my blasted arm I'd be in there doing it myself!" she tickles her faithful Jack Russell behind his ears and he leans back in rapture. Rapscallion, or Raps as we all call him, is actually the reason behind her slinged arm thanks to a rather over-excited lurch for a spaniel on Christmas Day. As invincible as Granny thinks she is, even she can't navigate the coast path with a frantic canine straining to warn off another dog.

"Go on!" she shouts, disrupting my reverie. "Swim for it!"

My brain shrieks as I bring my shoulders beneath the surface, every nerve ending gasping as wicked coldness swarms through my core. It prickles and resists, then just as suddenly as it started, the sensation dips leaving behind that wonderful sweet numbness that cascades through to the tips of my fingers the longer I tread water and familiarise myself. Emboldened, I adopt my trusty front crawl and sluice through the water, nudging along my yellow tub until I reach the other side. I emerge slick as an otter, exposed flesh blue with the effort of my veins to retain any source of heat. I don't feel it; instead the familiar burn prevails and I almost forget its January.

"Well done!" Her spell broken, Norah is cheering me wildly from across the water. Even Grace looks impressed.

I'm standing on a patch of golden sand that gets bigger with every wave, and for one glorious moment I'm completely alone with only the cry of seagulls in the distance and the roaring of the North Devon sea. I close my eyes and I'm transported to my happy place, my hidden haven, my home.

My hand closes around the spade and I rake at the sand, perhaps with the same urgency a visiting pig did all those years ago. However instead of a truffle, I'm searching for a much greater treasure – at least in my family's eyes. I brush against familiar roughness and my thumbs seek out the curved edges and walnut-shaped lump, unearthing it for inspection. Delighted, I give it a quick rinse and gaze upon my find. My first cockle of the season!

For the next twenty minutes my attention is dedicated to the digging, scrabbling and scooping of dozens of cockles. It's hard work but rewarding, and I soon lose myself in my efforts. The winter sun emerges from behind the clouds, sparkling across the dull-grey waves in the distance as they make their descent somewhere seemingly far away – at least until the tide turns.

By the time my tub is sufficiently full, the pool has reduced enough for me to wade back with it in my arms, swilling with seawater to keep the cockles alive until we can preserve them later. Grace meets me with a second empty tub.

"Care to swap?" I grin and she grunts. Granny nods approvingly. High praise indeed.

Dig, scrabble, scoop; my yields are similar, and I'm able to find clusters of cockles in droves. Granny is right; today was a good day for sea foraging.

It's a strange procession back up the cliff and along the steep hillside to Mortehoe. Two baffled sheep pause their day-long feasting to watch us warily from a safe distance, entranced by Norah who, with her marvellous rainbow bonnet, takes the lead with her bucket aloft, followed by Raps at her ankles, then Granny marching with her bad arm wrapped under her shawl. Grace and I follow behind, slowed by the weight of the tubs.

Luckily Granny's little house isn't far. Tucked amongst a string of traditional beach houses facing out to the coast, her tiny cottage is so inconspicuous you could easily miss it. Behind the red-brick exterior is a curious narrow property bestowed with a ginormous chimney flume. This takes up most of the living space, leaving just enough room for Granny's many shelves, her two worn, pink armchairs and a small dining table. A serving hatch reveals the miniscule kitchen that is more of a pantry, and the old storehouse behind. This is her pickling room and consists of a single bench, a Belfast sink and rows upon rows of jars lined up opposite. Half are empty, pristine and sterile, the other filled with pickled offerings ready for sale.

Grace and I gently place the tubs on the floor next to the sink, lifting each one in turn to rinse the cockles before leaving them to soak in salty water overnight.

"Can we eat some now?" Norah asks hopefully. She's a big fan of shellfish.

"Not yet," Granny says. "First we soak the sand out, then the real hard work begins." She ignores my raised eyebrows.

Dinner is fish and chips wrapped in newspaper, just like they are supposed to be, and mugs of Bovril straight out of my childhood – followed by Ambrosia rice pudding for extra nostalgia. Then it's up the steep cottage-style stairs to bed. The first-floor landing is where Granny's bedroom is with her single bed and sink, and a ladder leads up to the loft room where the girls and I are staying. The 'observatory' we call it, and the girls adore it. They don't seem to mind the fact that the toilet and shower are all the way back downstairs next to the kitchen, making middle-of-the-night loo dashes rather hair raising. They don't mind the old dusty floorboards and creaky radiator. As far as they are concerned, the room is a wonderful retreat with cosy cushions, blankets and scattered throws to sprawl on while they peer through the binoculars and spy on the hotel and rows of houses below.

"Mum, how did Granny and Grandpops both live here? It's so small!" Norah asks.

"In those days they didn't need TV's, loads of clothes and all the gubbins you both need," I tease. "Nanny used to sleep in this bedroom, and they just had a bigger bed."

"Did Nanny pickle cockles too?"

My imagination springs to life and I can picture my mother as a young girl in waders following her mother and father, stick primed and ready in one hand and a bucket clasped in the other.

"I like to think she did, don't you?"

Downstairs, I can hear the rasps of Granny's snoring, and I can picture her frail chest rising and falling like an indignant robin, chest puffed assertively.

"Will we talk to her tomorrow?" Grace rubs her eyes.

"Not yet. We promised her one more season, didn't we love."

Tomorrow, we'll wake up when the sky is still dark and watch the winter sun rise through the window, sending red and gold beams across the ceiling. We'll fill the house with loud bickering as we prepare for the day ahead, pulling on jumpers and arguing over the hot water. We'll have bacon and eggs around the tiny table and make Granny roar laughing with the girls' wit. Perhaps we'll even manage a quick beach walk before preparing for the day ahead.

We'll sit Granny on her stool and stand shoulder-to-shoulder, checking each cockle and discarding any dead ones. We'll thoroughly clean them and pop them in a pot to steam for five minutes. Once cool, we'll sort them and pluck them from their shells before tumbling them back into the pan with clove, all spice and mace. The giant bottles of white vinegar will be pulled out from under Granny's cockle bench and poured over the concoction, and the old cooker will gently bring it to the boil.

The girls will be shooed from the kitchen but the scent will still fill the house and our eyes will prickle slightly from the sharpness of the simmering vinegar. While the cooling process takes place, we'll return to the beach and cockle collecting will resume, ready for another day.

Finally, the end of the week will arrive and Dan will come to load his van with the very last collection of Hoswell's Heritage Cockles to distribute to the local deli and farm-shop counters. They'll be the last ever batch of pickled cockles to grace the tables of Granny's loyal following, and perhaps the palates of a few curious customers who want to try a local delicacy before it disappears forever.

Then there will be paperwork and sorting – so much sorting. The exchange of promises and money for beloved items. The most loved will be rounded up and transferred to the brand new private room with sunshine yellow walls and views of a different beach. It's difficult to picture the old, rough velvet chairs positioned in front of any other window but Granny's. It's unbearable to know that this historic home will soon be empty, devoid of footsteps echoing up the stairs and only shadows of years gone past will pass through the vacant rooms. I hope the next owners are kind, but I foresee modern heating, hot tubs and double glazing in the not-so-distant future.

The girls and I will return to suburbia, to the house with the red front door and muddy wellington boots on the doorstep: our home. Its Victorian-tiled hallway is full of dusty shoes and spiders' webs, the banister worn from years of children thundering down the stairs and sliding grubby hands along the wood. We'll be greeted, no doubt, by a slightly fraught father/husband, whose hair needs cutting and clothes need pressing – but who did a tremendous job of manning the fort nonetheless. The girls will be cornered by their excited little brother, wise for his seven years, who had to remain home with the chicken pox but hopes for a holiday gift and stories of sea monsters. Less keen on our return will be the chubby old tortoiseshell cat who, I'm sure, will have seized the moment and slept on every single bed for the sheer fun of it while I wasn't around to shoo her off.

Meanwhile, back in North Devon, Cockle Cottage will become just a name, perhaps with the old Hoswell's sign left above the door for a touch of shabby chic. Slowly, its history will retreat behind its old walls as its interiors become lavish and sleek with chalk paint and modern fixtures and fittings. I hope that traces will prevail; perhaps the lingering hint of pickling vinegar will creep into the new owners' nostrils now and again, or the sound of a pot simmering will dance on their ear drums.

That future looms ever closer – but first, there is work to be done. Cockle pickling is the family business, after all.

* * *

Author's disclaimer: although I have researched cockle-preserving for the purpose of this story, this account is purely fictional and I cannot confirm that Grunta Beach is a good spot for cockle harvesting.

Author Biographies

Val Allsup

Val has lived in Devon for ten years with her husband, her son, and various pets. Her real job is as a vet, but she decided to use the countless hours sat in playgrounds with her son to good use and try her hand at writing a story. Once you've read her tale you'll realise her mind didn't stray far from the playground for inspiration!

Ralph Bell-Ley

Ralph Bell-Ley was born in beautiful North Devon, where he lives with his family and his much-loved fur family. A long-time aspiring author, he achieved a Diploma in Creative Writing as a mature student and is working towards transforming years of creative ideas into fun picture books for children.

Caroline Berry

Caroline was born and raised in North Devon, she left once but she found it too 'peopley'. She lives in Ilfracombe with her family and a mini zoo.

Jane Bheemah

Janes grew up in Starcross, on the River Exe, close to Powderham Castle. The oak tree in *Under the Spreading Oak* stands in the deer park set in the grounds. Jane often enjoyed walks there and wondered, if trees could speak, what fascinating tales they'd have to tell!

She has had several short stories published over the years as well as two novels published under her pen name, Kathryn Haydon, both medical romances set in Devon, as befits a retired nurse.

- *Making the Difference*
- *Prognosis Guarded*

Darren Colwill

Darren is new to writing. At thirty-three years old this has been only his second try at a short story competition. He has always enjoyed stories and been a big fan of the fantasy genre. His favourite authors are Roald Dahl and Terry Pratchett. Being dyslexic, though, has historically hampered his confidence to write. But a strange imagination lies within him and bursts out on paper once in a while.

Nathalie Denzey

Nathalie has loved books, stories, and words for as long as she can remember. In her spare time she runs a writers' group where all sorts of stories are shared and told. Having studied creative writing and publishing, she volunteers for Read Easy, the fantastic adult literacy charity. She lives in East Devon. And is convinced she has a whole novel inside her.

Ella-Jane Hobson

Ella-Jane has had an interest in writing since they were a young child, over the years dabbling with stories of all lengths, poetry, and blogging. This is the first physically published piece of work that they have been a part of, but hopefully it won't be the last as they have plans to progress into novel writing, alongside the work that has been published online.

Maria Kinnersley

Maria began writing some years ago following her early retirement from her work in local government. She has had a few non-fiction articles published but this is her first foray into fiction. She is currently working on an anthology of short stories.

Katie Mallett

Katie is an Essex girl by birth. For twenty-three years she lived on Canvey Island. She began writing after the birth of her sixth child, taking inspiration from her surroundings and the joys and trials of motherhood. She was a regular contributor to Wake up to Wogan on BBC Radio 2

She moved to Ilfracombe in 2005, fulfilling a desire to feel the 'bones of England' beneath her feet. Ilfracombe has plenty of 'bones' and hills, features lacking in Canvey. Katie continues to write prose and poetry, from the comic to the macabre, as well as painting.

Damien Mansfield

Damien was born in 1985 and is still alive. He has lived in Devon for thirty years, primarily in the north.

For his sins, he has three children with his fiancée of twelve years. He has been writing short stories for his own pleasure for twenty years, but this is Damien's first published work outside of his primary school newsletter.

Lalla Merlin

Lalla sent two biographies, one of which was written by her daughter. We felt that both had merit and deserved to be included.

Lalla Merlin is a very small woman, who makes up for this fact by using as many foul words as she can and wearing obscenely big boots. She lives in Devon, with a series of bad dogs and the crippling weight of her anxiety. Sometimes, she eats a boiled egg. On Sundays, she rides a horse that is just as foul-tempered as she is, and follows a strict diet of things that begin with the letter B. There is a legend in the village where Lalla Merlin lives claiming that she is not, in fact, a woman, but a series of haunted owls in a trench coat.

Or

Lalla Merlin read English at Oxford University. As an undergraduate, she published poetry in several publications, and wrote for the university paper, *Cherwell*. She has written for Rowan Pelling's *The Amorist, Mslexia, Pony* Magazine, and *Museums Today*, among other publications, as well as her work as a journalist in the global attractions sector. She lives in North Devon with a pet wolf, and an assortment of feral family members.

Alex Morrison

Alex Morrison is a former journalist who worked for local newspapers and the BBC. He now writes about science for the University of Exeter and is writing a non-fiction book about journalism and a novel set in Antarctica.
You can connect with him on Twitter using @alexmorrison81

Jade Ruby

Jade is a passionate copywriter with a penchant for puns and an uncanny ability to make the driest of subjects sound rip-roaringly exciting – a handy skill for her line of work. She is relatively new to the world of creative writing despite dabbling since childhood, but she hopes to become a published author in one of her favourite subjects: drag, motherhood, or the paranormal.

When she isn't using her talents for the good of the NHS, she is making elaborate (bonkers) crafts with her three young children and having adventures across North Devon.

Colin Smith

Colin has read voraciously all his life and has written stories since the age of eight. His first successes as a writer were having stories printed in his primary school's newsletter, since when (and much later) he has also been published in two anthologies, small-circulation magazines and the September 2001 edition of *Devon Life*. In October 2013, he was awarded second prize in the North Devon Biosphere B10 writing competition. He also has a collection, *Writing The Bible And Other Rubbish*, available on Kindle, and a completed novel, *Murder At St Marmaduke's*, which can be read on his website, www.colin-z-smith.com.

You can also read more of Colin's writing in the following anthologies:

- *Seaglass and other poems and stories, ISBN 978-1-326-22901-6*
- *Mystery, Magic & Mayhem, ISBN 978-1-911438-53-3*

Irene Sugden

Irene Sugden lived in London for most of her life. Since her childhood, she predominantly based her passion for writing on observations and life experiences while growing up in the city. A few years ago Irene moved to North Devon. This new chapter in her life has inspired her to broaden her creativity horizons through her writing, fully embracing this beautiful part of the country.

Oliver J Tooley

Olli started this whole thing, Blue Poppy Publishing, back in 2016 so he could look like a published author. Here we are six years later with dozens of titles in print and now operating like a traditional publisher, rather than a self-publishing imprint. Olli has written several children's books (although they are the kind that adults can enjoy) and several more for adults and young adults. See the Blue Poppy Publishing website for details.

A selection of books and series by Oliver:

- *Children of the Wise Oak - & series*
- *For Cats' Eyes Only - & series*
- *John the Minstrel*
- *Time Tunnel to Londinium - & series*

Pamela Vass

Pamela was born and brought up close to London before moving to the West Country to study for an MA at Exeter University. Feeling very much at home, she decided to stay, only later discovering that her ancestors came from Devon. A strong sense of belonging had spanned the centuries.

Pamela enjoys sharing the stories behind her books and welcomes invitations from groups to speak, either in person in the south-west or UK-wide via Zoom.

Much of the inspiration for her books - both fiction and non-fiction - comes from the landscape and people of the West Country. There are always rumours to unearth, as with *Seeds of Doubt*, family dynamics to explore, as with *Shadow Child,* or unsung heroes to research, as with *The Power of Three* or *Breaking the Mould*.